The Five Steps of
Mr. Washington

A Novel
by

Christopher J. Moore

Clairvoyant Books Edition 2014

PO Box 2469
Winnetka, CA 91396

Library of Congress Control Number:
Library of Congress Cataloging – in – Publication Data

Christopher J. Moore 1971 –
The Five Steps of Mr. Washington
ISBN # 978-0-9728583-3-5

Manufactured in the United States of America

Visit our web site at http://www.clairvoyantbooks.com

Acknowledgments

I dedicate this book to all of the readers out there who support me and are fans of my books, and continue to ask when the next novel is coming out.

I would like to thank my mother and father, my two biggest fans. You are my example in life. May each book or television show I write make you more and more proud. I like to thank my wife Maricia and three kids, Jordan, Xavier and Christiahn who are the light of my life and keep me inspired. And, finally, all of my close friends and family: the Moores, Theards, and Biggs, the greatest family a guy could ask for. A special thanks to my big cousin Gary A. Theard Jr. Who taught me so much about business and life. May my work honor you always. Also a special thanks to Lyman Parrigin, for the copyedit job he did on my book. You are a special unique person who always teaches, inspires and puts people first above all. Very rare. Finally thanks to the professors at CSUN in the screenwriting department for their advice, wisdom, and friendship.

Christopher J. Moore has written two other novels—"God's Child" and Waiting For Mr. Right—and many screenplays and television shows.

The Five Steps of Mr. Washington

Chapter 1

THEODORE WASHINGTON SAT AT A CORNER TABLE next to a huge window in a high-rise at an exclusive restaurant in New York City. The city lights twinkled in the night as the rain fell hard. Lightning illuminated the inside of the restaurant.

Theo stared out of the window in a daze, thinking how he would be thirty-three in two months. Time was running out. He loved women and had many lovers in his life, but this was one situation he knew he couldn't fuck his way out of. This had to be resolved by the heart. The same heart that had sped up to the pace that had him sweating profusely, as he held an open box with an engagement ring inside.

He looked at the ring, his expression waning by the second. He sighed and shut the box.

Four months earlier, Theo lay in bed in a hotel room with a beautiful brown-skin woman with long straight hair. The hair was Indian but she wasn't. Their naked bodies glistened from the baby oil on the nightstand and the early morning sun that sliced through the curtains.

Theo stirred awake, blinded by the light of the sun. He looked at the gorgeous woman next to him, intertwined in satin sheets. On the back of her left shoulder was a tattoo that read *Coco*. He kissed her on her *Coco* softly. "Wake up sweetie." She smiled brightly as she came to.

"Man, I needed that. This bed is great," she said, licking her lips. "That's the best sleep I've had all year."

"This bed is comfortable," Theo said in agreement.

"Yes, it is." She stretched out her arms, arching her back to the max. Theo watched the covers fall to the small of her waist.

He liked how her body was toned, especially her long back and even longer legs. Her breast were b-cups, but her nipples were bigger than normal. And Theo loved them. They were the kind of nipples that would make any man drool a little, if he looked at them for more than a few seconds.

"Turn over, daddy, let me give you a back massage before I go."

"Is that all I'm gonna get?" he asked.

"Well, that depends on Mr. Johnson down there, Mr. Washington." She pulled the sheets all the way off, showing her beautiful long legs. Then she rubbed her breast and squeezed one of her nipples.

Theo smiled and wiped the drool off of his bottom lip. He flipped over onto his stomach.

She straddled him and started rubbing the back of his neck, working her way down. "God damn, girl! You are the fucking best."

"That's right, and don't you forget it."

He let out a deep sigh.

"Now turn over." He eased over, his erection making it a little difficult at first. He smiled.

She drained from him the little bit of fluid he had left, leaving him sprawled out on the bed helpless and weak. He stared at the ceiling wearing a big smile.

She put on her clothes and high heels, then put the rest of her things in a duffle bag. She looked at him lovingly and smiled. "All right, baby, I'm going to go." He remained on the bed, staring at the ceiling. "Theo? Theo?" she said, needing him to snap out of his wonderful trance.

"Oh, sorry. Bye." He gave her a smile. She smiled back.

"Well, are you going to pay me or what?"

"Excuse me?"

"Yeah, baby, it's not free."

"Oh. I thought you just liked me."

"I do. That's why I spent the night. What, do women always say 'let's get a room' to you?"

"No, but hey, it can happen."

"Well?" She smiled and so did he.

"Oh, my bad. Get the money out of my wallet; it's in my jeans. I trust you." He closed his eyes, in total bliss. She grabbed his jeans and pulled out his wallet. She extracted ten hundred-dollar bills, took five of them and put the rest back. "Don't forget to tip yourself," he said, still wearing a huge smile with his eyes closed. She shook her head, amused by his trusting nature.

"Thank you, baby," she said adoringly. She took an extra hundred-dollar bill and put her business card in his wallet. "Give me a call," she said as she sashayed out of the room.

Theo took a quick glance at his wallet on the nightstand then noticed the digital clock, which read 6:23 a.m.

The sun was shining but the rain fell harder and harder. Theo, dressed in sports attire, ran through a park at a fast pace. He was fit and looked great. He checked his watch, then picked up the pace. This was a part of his daily ritual. He ran five miles a day no matter what. Even in the rain. He loved running in the rain, because it made him feel that much more dedicated and more likely to accomplish his goals in life.

He looked at his watch again and picked up his speed. Nothing could stop him. He was thirty-two, handsome and driven. Most of all he was a man with a plan. For him, life was about working hard and getting results. His success in his career proved that.

After Theo finished his run, he drove home. His new 7 series *BMW* bobbed and weaved through traffic, and he eventually got a ticket. He didn't even care. He looked at his Rolex. He was running out of time. He continued to speed home.

Home was a spacious two-story Spanish-style villa. Beautifully landscaped. And a mailbox out front that read *Make It Happen*.

You could tell that Theo was anal just by the landscaping alone. Especially since he was a bachelor and it was just him living there.

He hopped out of his car, a towel wrapped around his neck, and jogged to the front door. He looked up to the sky, noticing the rain had subsided. He entered. The interior was just like the exterior. Perfect. The house was filled with art deco furniture, and hundreds of books were stuffed on the many shelves that lined the walls throughout the house.

He entered his study through two double doors. There were even more books. And a dry erase board covered with scribbled equations and formulas. Words like *success, goals, love, business, and planning* were prominent.

There were also lots of pictures and accolades everywhere. Some of the pictures were of him and other famous scholars, such as Tony Robbins, Cornell West, Dr. Phil, Deepak Chopra, Tavis Smiley, Oprah, and even a picture of President Barack Obama. Theo seemed to be a bit of a star fucker, even though he was considered a celebrity in his own right. Also on the wall behind his desk, was a picture of a mansion with several extravagant cars parked in front.

On his desk were dozens of Post-its, with things to do written all over them. He also had two books on his desk with Post-its throughout the pages. One was *Five Steps To Accomplish Your Goals* and the other was *Five Steps To A Happy, Fruitful Life*. Both written by him, with a pretentious picture of him on each cover.

He checked the messages on his phone. The voicemail beeped and a man with a Spanish accent spoke. "Hey, Theo, it's David. I've booked two book signings the second week of September, so have your ass ready. Also, you're scheduled to be on *The View* next week." The voicemail beeped.

He went to his life chart, which stretched out across the wall of his office. If anyone doubted that Theo was super anal, this chart was the proof. He checked his watch, then quickly went to a closet full of suits and grabbed one. There were tags on all of them, with the date and the TV show he wore them on. He quickly got dressed.

He looked in the full-size mirror and was pleased. He straightened his tie and rushed out.

Chapter 2

A MINIVAN PULLED INTO THE DRIVEWAY OF A BLUE house in Los Angeles, behind an old Buick that looked like it hadn't been driven in years. Palm trees stretched up to the sky, but these palm trees were distant cousins of the palm trees that Beverly Hills was known for. Some homes' front lawns were cut and landscaped. Some weren't. Some homes had a fresh coat of paint. Others peeled. But all the people who lived there were decent, hard-working folks.

Kim Jones was thirty-six, beautiful, but tired looking. She stepped out of the van, holding her forehead from the headache she'd had all morning.

"Kids, come on," Kim said. Lisa sixteen, Xavier seven, and Christiahn three. They got out of the van one by one. Xavier and Christiahn were fighting the whole time. "Will you two stop it!" Kim shouted. The kids stopped, but mad dogged each other. "Lisa, make sure Christiahn gets something to eat."

"Okay, mom."

"Mom, I miss daddy," Xavier said.

"Me, too, baby."

As Kim got some bags out of the van, she was distracted when an old man walked in front of her house with a dog on a leash. The dog took a dump on the front grass. The old man bent down with a plastic bag and a paper towel. However, a strong wind blew the plastic bag down the street. The man looked at the poop on the grass, then at the bag flying down the street. He played it off and started to walk away.

"I'm standing right here, Mr. Walker. I see you. You can tell me you're going to come back and pick that shit up." Frustrated, the old man waved her off and headed down the block.

Kim walked in the house and into the kitchen. "Xavier hurry up, you're gonna be late for school!" Kim could be heard throughout the house. Xavier hurried out of his room, grabbing his lunch as he flew by.

Kim handed the other bagged lunch to Lisa. Christiahn sat at the table eating cereal.

"More milk," she whined.

Lisa rolled her eyes and poured the last of the milk on her cereal.

"That's all the milk, Christiahn," Lisa said.

Christiahn gave a wry smile as she shoveled cereal in her mouth.

The front door opened.

"Grandma's here!" Christiahn shouted. Kim's mom Margie walked into the kitchen looking like an older version of Kim. She held two grocery bags.

"Hey, everyone."

"Grandma!" Christiahn shouted.

"Grandma, where were you? We went to daddy's burial sight," Xavier said.

"Yeah, where were you? It's his birthday," Christiahn added. Margie was thrown off. She felt horrible.

"I'm so sorry. I forgot," Margie said.

"It's okay, mom. We only stayed a few minutes," Kim said matter-of-factly.

"We brought him some flowers," Christiahn said, proud.

"Hey, Grandma," Lisa said. She kissed Margie on the cheek and headed to her room.

"I don't know why we couldn't just wait until this weekend. That way we could have stayed longer," Xavier said.

"Because today is his birthday," Kim answered.

"Was," Xavier said, as he walked out of the kitchen holding his sack lunch. Kim could feel his pain.

"Well, next time still call. I would have went with you," Margie said. Kim kissed her mother on the cheek.

"It's okay, mom." They both smiled.

"All right. Well, what do you want me to do?" Margie asked.

"Just stay with Christiahn while I drop off the other two." Kim looked around. "C'mon guys!" Kim grabbed her keys and headed out. Margie felt for her daughter as she dragged herself out of the kitchen, looking tired and obviously stressed.

Kim entered the living room looking for her purse. She saw it on the nightstand and walked past the television, where Theo Washington just happened to be doing an interview. Lisa and Xavier emerged from their rooms ready to go.

Kim, Lisa, and Xavier rode in the minivan. Everyone was quiet. Lisa glanced at her mother. "Are you okay?" she asked.

"Yeah, why?"

"Because. You seem like you're losing it."

"I'm not losing it. Don't worry about me. You just take care of yourself," Kim said.

"Well, I just want you to know that I'm proud of you, mom."

"For what?" Kim replied.

"For taking care of all of us. Just let me know if you need me to do anything for you."

"Like I said, just take care of yourself," Kim looked in the rearview mirror at Xavier, who stared out of the window. "Xavier, you okay back there?"

"I'm fine, mom."

"You know if you need to talk about anything, just let me know."

"I know," Xavier said, still staring out of the window.

"Mom, can Kevin take me out tonight?" Lisa asked.

"Where?"

"Just to the movies. It's his birthday." Kim thought about it for a moment.

"All right. Just remember your curfew."

Lisa nodded.

"Kevin's a butthole," Xavier said nonchalantly.

"Xavier!" Kim said.

"You're the butthole!" Lisa shot back.

"You guys stop." Kim shook her head outdone. "But for the record, I do think Kevin's a bit of a prick." Lisa rolled her eyes. Kim and Xavier shared a smile via the rearview mirror.

Chapter 3

THEO WAS IN THE STUDIO DOING AN INTERVIEW FOR *Wake Up America*. He was being interviewed by Kathy Grey, the host.

Theo held up his book, in full swing. "When you follow these steps it not only puts you on track to be successful in business, but in life. Because it's not just about making money. People have to stop equating success with money."

"Theo, we have a surprise for you from one of your friends in the business. She says she already bought your new book and wants to congratulate you on it personally."

"Oh?" Theo said, intrigued. He wore a huge smile that immediately disappeared at the sight of Jordan Yikes, his ex-girlfriend. She was beautiful and tall, in her early thirties, and a best-selling author in her own right. She also wrote self-help books. Mostly from a relationship point of view.

Jordan shook Kathy's hand then kissed Theo on the cheek. They continued to smile, knowing this was not a pleasant visit.

"Some of you may already know Jordan Yikes from her best-selling book, *Can't Buy Love*."

"Thank you, Kathy, for letting me come on."

"No problem. It's always a pleasure."

"So, I just wanted to say congratulations to Theo on his new book. I'm not sure if people know it or not, but this is the seventh anniversary of your first book, the book that started it all." Jordan and Kathy applauded, along with the audience. Jordan presented him with a cake from a man offstage. The audience continued to applaud.

"Oh, for a second I thought it was his birthday," Kathy said.

"No, that's not for another six months, right, Theo?" Jordan said.

"Right," Theo replied, apprehensive.

"I just know how important your steps are, and how you stick to your plans no matter what," Jordan said, wearing a huge smile. Kathy chimed in.

"Well, that's the key to all of your books, that you have to write it down for yourself and not deviate from it. That's why your books work," Kathy said, selling his formula.

"Exactly," Jordan said with a malicious grin.

"Well, that is true," Theo said, unsure of his own words.

"Yeah, for example, in your first book, you wrote that you will be married by the time you're thirty-three." Theo's fake smile dropped.

"Well, sometimes you have to take things as they come."

"No, you said you should never deviate from your plan. No matter what. It's in your book. This is the basis for your whole paradigm for a successful life," Jordan said as she held up an old book, with a pretentious picture of him on the cover. Kathy looked on, loving the drama. "It's right in here on page ninety-eight." Jordan looked at the audience. "Now, ladies, are we going to let him off the hook?"

The ladies in the audience screamed, "No!" Theo smiled, waving for the women to settle down.

"But, hey, sometimes you have more important things to do. Let me tell you about my next book, I really want to…"

"No no no, we are not going to let you off the hook that easy," Kathy interrupted trying to contain her laughter.

"No, we're not," Jordan seconded.

"But, the…"

"Sounds like bull to me!" Jordan cut off Theo. The crowd erupted in laughter. Then chanted *bullshit*. The producers freaked, waving their hands to calm down while the crowd screamed *bullshit*. Jordan sat back in her chair, arms folded. Mission accomplished. Kathy calmed her audience down, loving every bit of it.

"So, are you going to be married by your thirty-third birthday?" Kathy asked.

Theo blinked several times, before swallowing the lump in his throat. "Yeah, if I wrote it. Absolutely." Jordan smiled at Theo. Theo smiled back with a *fuck you* behind it.

"Well, thank you, Jordan, for coming by and surprising our guest. And thank you, Theodore Washington, for visiting." The crowd applauded. Jordan grabbed a handful of cake and stuffed it in Theo's mouth, leaving cake all over his lips. Kathy's eyes went wide, wearing a fake smile. "You can get his new book in stores as of... today," Kathy said with a stunned expression. The three of them all presented their fake smiles for the camera, including Theo with cake around his mouth. The stage manager stood horrified, shaking his head.

"That's a wrap!" the stage manager yelled.

Jordan got up. "Payback's a bitch, lover boy." Theo watched her stomp off, feeling great about herself. He then looked at Kathy, who gave him a *yikes* expression.

As Theo drove, he banged on the steering wheel enraged while yelling into his cell phone. David, his friend and manager, was laughing hysterically, slamming his fist on the steering wheel of his Porsche. "That's hilarious!" David shouted, while his cousin's demo CD blasted Spanish music.

"It's not funny. She put me in a position where I have to get married."

"Theo, that's ridiculous. You don't have to get married."

"David, she used my first book to show that I promised, I will get married by thirty-three."

"Well then, find a wife."

"This calls for desperate measures. Come on man, tell me how to spin this thing. You're my manager."

"You can always say you're gay!" David laughed, banging on his steering wheel.

"I need help, David!"

"All right, I'm on it." Theo's frustration had peeked, giving his steering wheel a final smack.

Chapter 4

STUDENTS MILLED ABOUT THE UCLA CAMPUS, SOME heading to class while fraternities and sororities passed out flyers to their events. Theo breathed deeply, taking in the atmosphere. He smiled. He looked handsome, wearing jeans and a sports coat with loafers.

He entered into a jam-packed classroom full of eager students. As he made his way to the front of the classroom, the students applauded. "All right, everyone, settle down," he said, smiling. When he got to the podium, he looked over the class. "When the president of the university, asked me what subject I wanted to teach, first I thought trigonometry, havin' got my master's in mathematics. It's one of my favorite subjects. But then I asked myself, how could the students benefit the most from me being here? There are other mathematicians here well equipped to teach that subject." Students looked on, delighted. "So I asked, could I create my own curriculum? And he said yes." The students applauded. "One of the perks of having been on the Oprah show, I guess." The students laughed. Two beautiful girls in the front row flirted, smiling at him. He smiled back. "So, this class—as most of you may already know—is about life organization." Theo wrote and underlined *life organization* on the chalkboard. "And how not to waste steps on your way to creating a complete and happy life. But, follow five essential steps and you can be anything you want to be. Know what you want to do in your career. Know whether you want to be rich or just make enough money to be comfortable. Some of you students will be going to law school only to find that you just want to be a stay-at-home mom… or dad." Students laughed. "These are things that you need to know. I have so many friends who go to law school, pass the bar, then realize they want to be actors. Which means they end up waiting tables with a hundred-thousand-dollar student loan." Students continued to laugh. "And we all know you don't need a law degree to be an actor." Even Theo had to give a chuckle to that one. "So, these are the things that I want you to think about while you're in my class. How to make each moment count. How to make the most out of your life. From your goals in your career to the goals in your own personal life. So let's begin. Because the clock is ticking." Theo smiled. "Plus I got a date tonight."

Chapter 5

THEO AND NINETEEN OTHER MEN STOOD ACROSS from twenty women in a banquet hall. The women wore beautiful dresses and the men wore suits. All of them wore nametags.

In the middle of everyone stood Sharon Haze. She was a bossy woman in her late forties, who wore a tight-fitted dress with her big boobs pushed up toward her chin. Plastic surgery was definitely in play, and she wasn't ashamed to say so. She would often tell people proudly, give them a feel, and go on and on about the procedure.

She smiled, seeing how nice everyone looked. "All right, ladies and gentlemen. Welcome to the exclusive, one-of-a kind, Premier Match Makers Club," she said in her own grand way. The men and women applauded. She spoke like someone's mother, talking to her children. "Now, as you all know, this is not about hooking up for one-night stands. And if that's what you're here for, there's the door. Because this is not about sex.

It's about finding love. True love. To find someone to spend the rest of your life with, and get married!" Everyone cheered. "Shall we begin?"

Speed dating ensued amongst the men and women, sitting at different tables. Theo sat at a table talking with the first woman. He had a list of questions on his notepad. She looked at the notepad and rolled her eyes. "So, let me ask you a series of questions." Theo said. The woman looked at him oddly, like he had some nerve.

"I didn't know I was being interviewed for a job." He smirked at her, not interested.

He sat across from another woman. She was beautiful but didn't look as polished as some of the other women. He thought about the last woman's reaction to his notepad, and discretely put it out of sight. She looked at him as though she recognized him. "You look familiar?"

Theo gave a cordial smile.

"I get that a lot." She smiled, ready to converse.

"You have to excuse my hair, but my hairdresser flaked on me, so I had to do it myself."

"Oh, no problem."

"So, what do you do?" he asked.

"I work in sanitation."

"Mmm, trash?"

"Yeah."

Theo instantly looked uninterested. She read his face and gave him a dirty look, then got up and walked away.

Theo sat across from another woman. "So, what do you do?" he asked.

"I'm a doctor," the woman replied. Theo sat up, interested. He smiled.

"A doctor?"

"Yeah."

"What's your specialty?"

"I'm a psychologist." His smile disappeared.

"So, you like to play head games," Theo said. She sat there staring at him as though they were playing chess.

"I don't know, do you?" she replied.

"See, you're playing head games already." Theo looked at her, no longer interested. She smirked and looked at the nametag on his breast pocket.

"Well that's what life is, Mr. Washington, an assortment of games."

"Well, that depends on who's..."

"Playing," she chimed in.

"Huh?"

"Huh?" she repeated. They stared at each other, confused.

"Huh?" they said at the same time.

Theo continued to talk with different women, not impressed with any of them.

The function was over and workers cleaned up the place, moving tables and chairs. Sharon and Theo talked. "Look, sweetie, you can't be so picky."

"Hey, I just know what I want. And I don't think that I should have to settle. I don't have time to waste, I'm on a schedule. I want to be married in six months."

"No one is asking you to settle. But nobody's perfect. You do understand that no person is perfect... You want to find a wife, right?"

"Yes, that's the plan."

"Well, you have to get to know the person and not worry about their flaws. And get rid of that list!" She snatched the notepad out of his hand and started to read "Beautiful, funny, bright teeth, nice butt, no kids, no cats... Look, you have to lighten up. No cats? I love cats." She was appalled by the list, as it continued on, page after page.

"I'm allergic to cats."

"Well, what was wrong with the woman who worked in sanitation? I liked her for you."

"You mean, trash?"

"Yeah."

"Well, I just kind of thought, we were from two different worlds."

"Why, because she doesn't have a Ph.D. or something? Let me let you in on a little secret. She owns the biggest sanitation company on the West Coast, and I'm pretty sure she makes about twenty times more than you." Theo looked like he might have missed an opportunity.

Chapter 6

THEO PARKED IN FRONT OF AN APARTMENT building in Los Angeles. He was dressed in a black tuxedo, looking suave and debonair. He looked at people gawk at his impressive BMW, as if it didn't belong. Across the street, people hung out drinking beer and playing dominos on their front porch. Theo turned off his engine, looked out of the passenger's window, and smiled. Coco strolled out of her building wearing a posh black gown. She looked stunning, standing almost six feet with her hills on. He hopped out and opened her door. They gave each other a kiss on the cheek. "You look... perfect," he said, impressed. He knew she would look gorgeous dressed up, but had no idea she would look like a supermodel.

"You don't look too shabby yourself," she said, excited about the night ahead of them. "And thanks for sending me the dress. I don't have to give it back, do I?" Theo smiled as if she did.

"No, it's yours. I'm just glad you weren't busy."

She carefully got in the car, not wanting her dress to get wrinkled. Theo closed her door and ran around to the driver's side, while glancing at his watch. He got in. "We're just a little bit late."

"Well hit it, boo."

"I love it when you call me boo." Theo smiled and drove off.

They walked into an industry party for people in media at the Beverly Hills Hotel. It was an elegant affair. There were several celebrities in the crowd, and a lot of rich people. Theo socialized, introducing his beautiful date to some of his peers. Tonight his beautiful date's name was not Coco, but Chanel Williams, her birth name.

They sat at a round table, listening to a speaker talk about where new media was headed over the next five years.

They also talked about where the self-help industry was gravitating toward. However, Theo missed a lot of it, distracted by Coco, who looked beautiful and chic. He was amused at the little secret that only he knew—that Chanel was really Coco. A wonderful girl from the hood in Atlanta, who was a prostitute. A woman who didn't have a PhD or law degree or MBA. But a woman who used to strip back in Atlanta, who came to Los Angeles to start over and pursue her dream of owning her own hair salon.

The speaker cracked a joke and Coco laughed. Theo liked her smile. She had perfect bright white teeth. She also snorted a little when she laughed. He thought it was adorable.

As the night went on, and Theo strategically made all of the contacts he needed to make, they decided to leave.

On the drive home Theo talked about his new book and how competitive the self-help industry was becoming, and about his plan to really take his career to the next level. She talked about her goals as well, and how she planned to buy her own salon within a year. Then expand to other businesses. She told him that at the end of the day she wanted to be a businesswoman. He could tell she was daunted by the task, but determined to make it work.

"It'll happen, you'll see," Theo said.

"I know. I just want it to happen sooner than later."

"It will. Remember, it's about the journey not the destination."

"Have you forgotten? My journey is kinda fucking people."

"Oh, yeah." They shared a laugh. "You know, you're not just beautiful, you're also smart. And one day you'll realize that you can do anything if you put your mind to it. Just remember that."

"I hear you, Theo," she said, not taking it to heart.

"You'll see. One day all of the stars will align and you'll realize your true purpose."

"I hope so. To be honest, I'm kind of getting tired of the... you know."

"You are?"

"Yeah."

"So does that mean I'm going to have to find real dates for this kind of stuff?" Theo asked with a smile. She gave a little laugh.

"Maybe."

"You know, when I met you, all I could think about was how beautiful you were."

"Well, you were easy on the eyes, too," she said, wearing a smile. "So, do you want to have a nightcap?" Coco asked with seductive eyes. "It's on the house." Theo's eyes went wide.

"I would love to, but I have to wake up early tomorrow."

"Well, too bad for you," she sang, taunting him with her words. Theo groaned, glancing at her.

"Yeah, too bad for me."

Theo pulled up in front of Coco's apartment building and parked. They looked at each other, feeling the tension. Theo leaned in and kissed her on the cheek. He couldn't resist, and went for the lips. She stopped him, gently putting her hand over his mouth.

"No. You're not going to get me all hot and bothered and leave me high and dry. Now give me my money so I can go upstairs and take care of myself," she said amused.

"Wow," he said almost in pain at the thought of her *taking care of herself.* "You're killing me…" She smiled. They got out of the car and Theo walked her to the front door.

"You're missing out," she sang, with a laugh. Theo returned her smile with an *I know* expression. He fished inside his pocket and pulled out a roll of hundred-dollar bills, wrapped in a rubber band.

"Thanks," he said as he handed her the money, as if he was paying up on a bet.

"My pleasure, boo."

She kissed him on the cheek goodbye, using a little tongue. He smiled as she turned around, went inside and closed the door. Theo dropped his head in total conflict with himself, contemplating whether to knock or go home. But something just didn't feel right about it. So he sucked it up and went home.

Chapter 7

KIM COOKED WHILE THE KIDS DROVE HER CRAZY, fighting and chasing each other around the house.

Margie helped with the kids as best she could, while Kim's anger continued to escalate until she couldn't take it anymore. She slammed a spoon down on the counter. "Will you guys stop running in here? Fuck!"

"He took my sucker!" Christiahn cried out.

"No I didn't, I found it!" Xavier shouted back.

"I hate Xavier!"

"Stop it! Both of you, just stop it!" Kim screamed. Everyone froze. She looked down at her hands shaking. She took a deep breath. "Go wash your hands and get ready for dinner," Kim said, almost as if she was startled by her own voice. The kids left, spooked. Margie noticed Kim's hands shaking.

"Are you okay?" Margie asked. Kim took a moment. She tried to calm herself down, taking in deep breaths, hoping not to pass out.

"No, mom, I'm not. I'm losin' it. I'm drownin' here. I got bills that if I even think about, make my head hurt. I hate my jobs. I mean it's easier when you're here, but you're not all the time. Lisa helps, but..." Kim took a moment, a lump in her throat preventing her from continuing. Then with a hard swallow, "Why did God take my husband?" She broke down crying.

"Come here, baby," Margie said. Kim approached her mother.

"It's all just too much. I don't know what I'm gonna do." Margie hugged Kim as she sobbed uncontrollably.

Lisa stood out of view by the doorway, tears running down her face as her mother bawled in her grandmother's arms.

Kim's head lay in her mother's lap on the couch. The kids were asleep and the house was quiet. Kim was extremely relaxed, having had five shots of tequila. Something her mother bought her to take the edge off. She wondered what would become of her life. And how she was going to get herself out of her predicament. She had two jobs she hated. Kids that she couldn't afford. This was a life she never thought she would have. Not in a million years. She was a woman who wanted to have two kids, then go back to school and finish getting her degree and become a successful businesswoman in the medical profession. But since her husband made a good enough living, she enjoyed being a stay-at-home mom. Now she had to do it all.

"I'm tired, mom. I mean, I'm really tired."

"I know you are. But it will get better. Just trust in God."

"I know."

"You know what you need? You need to go to church with me."

"Mom, I'm too tired to go anywhere."

"Well, let me know when you wanna go."

"I will."

"I deposited two hundred dollars into your account by the way."

Kim looked up at her mother.

"Mom, you didn't have to do that."

"I wanted to. I decided not to give it to the church this month and give it to you. I'll make it up next month." Kim let out a sigh, already thinking about what bill to pay with it.

"Thanks, mom."

"Pastor did a whole sermon on tithing yesterday, too, so I felt a little bad."

"Well don't."

"Tithing is good."

"I know. I just don't believe everything they're selling. I don't believe in you giving two hundred dollars to the church if the pastor is driving a three-hundred-thousand-dollar Bentley."

"It's a Maybach, and the church brought it for him."

"Then he should have given it back. People are out of work, homeless and starving, and the pastor is questioning people's commitment to their faith about tithing, while he lives in a mansion. Please." Margie's eyes ran from Kim's, knowing their history on the subject.

"Well, I can't be responsible for pastors or churches or anybody. That's on them. All I can be responsible for is me. So when I tithe, hey, I did my part. The rest is on them and their souls."

Kim thinks about her words.

"Changing the subject. Why don't people tell you that having kids isn't what it's all cracked up to be? And basically it sucks. I mean it really does suck," Kim said, laughing. Margie looked at her like she was losing it. "All they think about is their selves. They're loud, obnoxious, self-centered. Stinky. Messy. And they don't listen. By the time they're grown, I'm gonna be a crazy woman. I mean really batshit crazy. Like screaming at cars driving by kinda crazy." They both laughed.

"No, you're not."

"Yes, I am. And I think these kids aren't even going to help me. They're just going to drive on by, embarrassed."

"Well, I won't."

"You promise? Because it's just us. We can't depend on them in there. All we got is us."

"Okay, you need to go to sleep now."

"Maybe they're my punishment for not going to church anymore."

Margie laughed and popped Kim in the face with a pillow.

"Go to sleep."

"Okay. But you promise not to drive by…"

"Sleep."

Margie rubbed Kim's head, staring down at her baby, wishing she could do something to help her. Kim's eyes slowly closed and she went to sleep in her mother's lap. Margie continued to stroke her head.

Theo ran full speed at a park. This wasn't his normal running spot, but he was driving by it one day and liked the trail.

His eyes showed his determination as he ran to exhaustion. A beautiful woman ran toward him with the same determination. He was thrown off by her big boobs bouncing up and down and ran straight off a ten-foot drop. "Ahhh!" Theo yelped as he tumbled down.

He lay at the bottom of the hill for a moment, catching his breath. Once he realized he was all right, he had to laugh. He looked around, hoping that no one saw him. But there was an old lady sitting on a bench, staring at him. She shook her head as if she were looking at the last moron. He gave her a smile, then got up and dusted himself off.

He climbed back up the hill, dirt and grass stains all over him. He looked around, embarrassed, and resumed his jog.

He continued to push himself all the way to a water fountain. He caught his breath, then started to drink. He drank until he heard a woman's voice behind him. "Excuse me," the voice said.

Theo turned around, water dripping from his goatee.

Her name was Whitney Mansfield. Twenty-eight with a golden brown complexion, beautiful and sophisticated. She stood there with her hands on her hips, breathing hard, dressed in sports attire that showed off her six-pack. "Are you done?" she asked, looking at him with curiosity.

He looked her up and down. He liked what he saw.

"Well, to be done requires me to remove my lips from the water."

She rolled her eyes, slightly irritated.

"Well, please hurry so I don't have to pass out, out here."
He stepped away from the fountain. He stared at her butt as she
bent over to drink. He was impressed. She had the body of a
track and field sprinter.

She took as long as he did. He was amused. He stood
there until she was finished. "So, do you always pop out of
nowhere like the water police?" She did a double-take.

"Do I know you?" she asked.

"I don't think so," Theo replied.

"Wait a minute, you're Theodore Washington." He
smiled, appreciating the recognition.

"That's me."

"Yeah, I saw you on the Oprah Show."

"You saw that? I hope I didn't look too bad."

"Only when you tried to tell her why she wasn't
married."

"Yeah, my manager said that wasn't the best move. I was
just trying to make a point."

"You made a point all right. Never to be on her show
again." She laughed. He gave a little chuckle.

"So, what's your name and what do you do?"

"I'm Whitney Mansfield and I'm an attorney."

"A lawyer, huh?"

"Yep." They stood there smiling at each other. Interested.

Chapter 8

THEO AND WHITNEY SAT IN A SPORTS BAR
watching a basketball game and drinking beer.

"Thanks for watching the game with me. The Lakers are
my team," Theo said.

"My team, too," Whitney replied, looking more into the
game than him. They cheered at the same time. Theo gave her a
look, impressed. They both smiled.

"Can I ask you a question?" he asked with a serious
expression. Whitney hesitated for a moment, thrown off by the
sudden change in mood.

"Sure, what is it?"

"It's a serious one."

She looked at him strange.

"Go ahead," she replied.

"Will you marry me?" Theo said, playfully.

She spit out her beer, amused.

"Excuse me?"

"Will you marry me?"

She cracked up. He laughed as well.

"No. I just met you."

"Hey, you're single. I'm single. I figured, what the hell?" They stared at each other as though they were trying to figure each other out. They chuckled.

"You are crazy," Whitney said with a curious smile.

"No I'm not. You're just that beautiful. Plus I'm on a schedule. So let's just zip on down to Vegas and do this."

She blushed.

"Look, I'm not zipping anywhere with you."

"Don't like the Vegas thing? You want the big wedding, with four hundred of your closest friends?" he said with a sarcastic grin. She smiled, charmed.

"Actually, I prefer a Vegas wedding when I get married. I've never wanted the big, unnecessary party. For me it's always been a waste of time and money. But back to your wonderful proposal; it's no because I don't know you."

"Oh, I get it. Playing hard to get." They laughed.

"Well, first let me ask you, scholar boy, do you always pick up strange women at parks? Then propose to them on the first date?"

"No. Do you always harass people at water fountains?"

"Only when they're trying to break a record like you were."

"I was thirsty."

"So was I."

"Yeah, I noticed. You drank more than I did."

"Whatever," she laughed off.

Theo stared at her playfully, nodding his head as if he had her all figured out.

"I can see this isn't going to work already. I'd like to rescind my proposal."

She laughed.

"Like I said, whatever," Whitney said, amused.

"Whatever," Theo mocked, wearing a big smile. They looked at the game on the television and cheered at the same time.

She blushed.

"So why is a successful, fairly handsome man like yourself not already married?"

Theo thought about it.

"I tend to stay really busy. And I'm always jumping on a plane to go somewhere."

"Well, when was the last relationship you were in?"

"Serious relationship. Oh, about three years ago. She was an actress."

"An actress?" Whitney was intrigued.

"I didn't know she was an actress at first. I accidentally found her headshots under her bed and broke up with her immediately."

"No, you didn't!"

"Yes, I did. I don't do actresses."

She laughed.

"Not like that. It's just actors tend to not be the most stable people in the world."

"So what about lawyers?" she asked, giving him her full attention.

"Lawyers? Well the fact that someone can go to law school, pass the bar. You did pass the bar, right?"

"Of course." Whitney smiled.

"See. It shows that they can commit to something."

"You're funny."

"It's a gift." Theo's cell phone rang. He pulled it out and scanned the number, then cut it off.

"If that's one of your ladies, feel free to answer it."

"It's not. It's actually my cousin, Sam."

She smiled, not sure if she believed him.

"Can I be honest with you?" she asked.

"Sure."

"I looked you up on the Internet."

"You did?"

"Yeah. And I have to say I'm impressed," she said, matter-of-factly.

"Well, thank you." Theo smiled at the compliment. "So how come you're not married with kids, with the house, and the white picket fence?"

"Too busy like you, trying to be partner I guess. But, those things are definitely in the plan."

"So is that a *yes* to my proposal? Because, like I said, I'm on a schedule."

She snickered.

"I'm on a schedule, too. But the answer is still no, scholar boy." She laughed, charmed, as they continued to drink.

Chapter 9

KIM SCURRIED AROUND THE OFFICES IN A HIGH-RISE, trying to clean windows as fast as she could so she could rush to her second job cleaning motel rooms. She was tired. It had been over a year and a half since her husband passed. And she had been keeping up this hectic schedule ever since.

She scrubbed a huge window overlooking the city, but her cleaning came to a halt at the sight of her reflection. Her hair had come loose and looked wild and unkempt. To her, the reflection in the glass looked like a different person. A person who had lost herself.

She thought about when she and her husband were high school sweethearts, and he was all she had ever known.

They met when they were in the tenth grade in homeroom. She always thought that he was silly and didn't think much of him. He hung with a group of guys who were practical jokers. Always pulling someone's chair out, making them fall. Or stealing teachers' chairs and leaving them out by their cars.

He was all jokes and laughs, until one day he got home and found his mother dead on the kitchen floor. She had a brain aneurysm and died trying to get to the phone to dial 911.

From that point on he was a different person. He had to live with his grandmother, who was a wonderful woman. She was stern and would not tolerate any bad behavior. She told him to step up to the plate and make his mother proud. So that's what he did. He improved in school, making the dean's list, and got himself a job working after school in a local supermarket.

Everyone at their school knew what happened with his mother, and everyone felt sorry for him. Including Kim.

One day Kim was in the library sitting at one of the tables when she heard a voice behind her ask, *Is anyone sitting here?* She turned around and it was him. *Thomas Jones*. It shook her for a moment. She then noticed how crowded the library was and how the seat was the only one available. She replied, *No one's sitting here.* He sat in the chair across from her, opened up his backpack and took out a book. From that moment on they were inseparable.

Lisa rode with her boyfriend, Kevin, thinking about what her mother said about him. She knew he could be a jerk at times, but she liked him anyway. He was charming and cute. And most of all ambitious. He was always throwing parties at different people's homes and wanted to eventually buy his own club. She knew he would be successful. It was just a matter of time.

His pride and joy was his 1976 Mustang, which he thought was the fastest car in the world. He would race anyone who challenged him. The car was worth about two thousand dollars, and the rims, alarm, and sound system together were worth about four thousand. He loved the attention the car got him, always nodding his head coolly to the music as the ladies watched him drive by. In his mind he was already a star.

But the one thing that Lisa appreciated most about Kevin, was his way of making her feel like she was the only girl in the world when they were together. He would tell her he loved her obsessively. And she would tell him she loved him as well, even though in her heart it felt like a hard *like*. "Thanks again for the hat," Kevin said, looking in his rearview mirror at the black suede fedora he was wearing.

"I'm glad you like it. I was worried that it wouldn't fit."

"Well, it fits."

"So where are we going?" she asked.

"It's a surprise." He gave a sly smile.

"A surprise ey'," she said, curious.

"Yeah," he said, matter-of-factly. "You look pretty."

She looked at him wearing a big smile, starry-eyed.

"Why you being so nice?" Lisa asked, suspicious.

"What are you talking about? I'm always nice."

"You always tell me you love me, but you're not always nice."

"You know I'm nice, in every way." He pulled up in a motel parking lot. She looked up at the big sign in front, with a picture of a fox.

"Typical," she said with a smirk.

"What do you mean, typical? I see that smile on your face."

"Hey, it's all good," she continued to smile.

"I know it's all good," he said, showing his dimples. He reached in the backseat and pulled out a black plastic bag. He gave a little chuckle and handed it to Lisa.

"What's this?"

"Open it."

"I'm scared to," Lisa said, hesitant, starting to giggle. Finally she rolled her eyes, then opened it. It was sexy red lingerie. It also came with a small horsewhip. She was taken aback. "Okay, you are trippin'!"

"What, it's my birthday," he said, smiling so hard his dimples were like holes in his cheeks.

"Nothing," she said amazed by his audacity.

"Let's go," he said, eager.

When they entered the room, Lisa looked around. She thought to herself that it wasn't that bad, for a motel that rented by the hour.

Kevin put his things on the bed and came up behind Lisa. He hugged her softly and kissed her on the back of her neck. It sent shivers down her spine. Her neck was extremely sensitive and he knew it. "You going to put that on for me?"

"I don't know."

"What do you mean you don't know?"

"Fine. I'll put it on. Don't act so desperate." She nudged him off of her playfully. She grabbed the bag with the lingerie in it and went into the bathroom.

Kevin reached into his backpack and pulled out his phone. He set it on the nightstand and took off his clothes except his underwear. He acted like a kid getting ready for Santa Claus to come down the chimney.

"Are you ready?" she asked from the bathroom.

"Yeah," he answered, eager. He turned on his phone camera to record.

"Where did you get this shit from? It looks ridiculous." She eased out of the bathroom, embarrassed, wearing a red see-through gown with black thong panties and bra. The panties had a red heart in the front, with an arrow going through it.

She quickly covered her bra and panties with her hands, horrified that he was holding his phone, recording her. "Oh my God, what are you doing?" she shouted.

"I'm recording you, beautiful."

"Turn it off!" she said, irate.

"Why?"

"Because I said so!" She marched over to him and snatched the phone out of his hand.

"Why you trippin'?"

"You're the one that's trippin'." She turned it off and tossed it onto the bed, making it bounce right off and onto the floor.

"What the fuck!" He snatched his phone off the floor to make sure that it wasn't broken. He turned it on and off. "You could have broke my phone!"

"What are you thinking?"

"I just thought that we could have a little fun with it. Then erase it when we're done."

"You should have asked me first," Lisa said, calming down. Kevin continued to look his phone over. "Sorry about your phone." She thought that maybe she overreacted. "Is it okay?"

"Yeah, it's cool. Damn, girl, you gotta loosen up!" He chuckled.

"I am loose. I got this tramp suit on for you." They both laughed.

"What are you talking about? It's sexy."

"No it's not." She looked at herself in the mirror on the wall.

"Yes it is," Kevin said, staring at her reflection in the mirror. "All right, turn around and do a little dance for me so I can see what I paid for." He went to the nightstand and turned on some music on the clock radio. She looked at him as if he was pushing it, but then exhaled with a smirk. He turned the phone camera on and pointed it at her, wearing a huge smile.

"No." She pushed the camera out of her face.

"Please…" He pleaded, trying to be as charming as possible. "C'mon, girl, let's do something different and have a little fun."

She sighed again, cracking a smile and giving in.

"All right, but we're going to erase this shit before we leave." He smiled with his whole face.

"Cool," he said, scanning Lisa's beautiful figure with his camera phone. He then zoomed in on her beautiful smile.

Chapter 10

THEO KNOCKED ON THE FRONT DOOR OF AN OLDER well-kept two-bedroom house in Los Angeles. Sam Ross sat on the couch in the living room. He was forty-one, slightly overweight. And wasted. He was Theo's older cousin and best friend. Four empty beer cans and a half bottle of Hennessy were sitting on the coffee table. He looked at the door, moaned, then slowly got up and strolled over to answer it. "Who is it?"

"It's me," Theo said. Sam opened the door. "So what's up?" Theo asked, wearing a big smile.

"Don't you know how to answer your phone?"

Theo looked at him funny, noticing his words were slurred.

"I was on a date. Are you drunk? It's the middle of the day." Sam gave Theo a goofy smile.

"Yes, I am. And for good reason. Did you just say you were on a date?"

"Yep."

"A real date or that speed-dating crap?"

"A real date, asshole."

"With who?"

"This beautiful woman I met at the park. Man, she's perfect." Sam looked at him, skeptical. "I'm telling you, I think I found her. Matter of fact, I know I found her. She's Mrs. Washington."

"I thought you were taking a break from women after that crazy psychotherapist."

"I was, but now it's time for me to get married."

"Your anal ass finally ran out of time, ey'? Mister five steps to everything."

"Don't hate me because I plan things out."

"That's your problem, Theo. You think life is just one big-ass business plan. Well it's not, my friend. For example, like when I came home and my wife and daughter were gone. Just left me. And for what? A fucking magician that arches his eyebrows. What kind of shit is that? Oh, or when I went to work yesterday and they fired my ass after thirteen years…"

"You got fired?"

"Yep. Downsized out of the blue. Like the little bitch that could. Can you believe it?"

"I'm sorry, man. Are you okay, money wise?"

"I don't know."

"Well, how much you need?"

"I don't want any money from you."

"Sam, you're like my brother. If I got it, you got it."

"If I really need it, I'll let you know."

"Do me a favor. Let me send your daughter a little something on your behalf."

Sam was touched. His eyes welled up.

"I know she's in college and all," Theo said.

"I love you, man," Sam slurred and hugged Theo.

"Don't sweat it. You've had my back in the past. Hell, you practically put me up all through college."

Sam puked on Theo's shoulder. Theo's face turned sour.

"I bet you didn't plan that, did you?" Sam said.

Chapter 11

KIM'S KIDS PLAYED IN THEIR FRONT YARD WHILE Margie and Kim watched them from the front porch. Margie noticed Kim staring in a daze. "You okay?" she asked.

"I'm fine."

"Okay," Margie said, as if she wasn't going to ask again.

"What do you mean, okay?"

"Okay." Margie sipped her tea with her pinky out, making Kim laugh. Kim rolled her eyes and smiled at her mother.

Lisa strolled up to them, hesitant, biting her lip. "Mom, can I talk to you?"

"Sure, what is it?" Lisa took a moment before speaking. Kim sat up in her chair, realizing that this might be serious.

"I've decided that I'm not going to college right away."

"What?" Kim responded, head cocked, a crease across her forehead.

"I figured I could get a job and help you with the bills." Kim was taken aback. Margie looked on, touched.

"Listen, baby. Although I appreciate what you're trying to do, you don't have a choice. You are going to college right after you graduate. You got one more year and then—trust me—you're gone."

"But mom, I can wait…"

"No. It's not up for discussion," Kim said in a stern tone. Lisa turned and walked away toward her brother and sister.

"That was really sweet," Margie said. She looked at her granddaughter, impressed. "You guys did a great job raising her."

"She's a great kid," Kim added.

Lisa suddenly stopped walking. She put her hands on her hips, dropped her head and reeled around. She pulled a letter from her back pocket, sighed and marched back up to the porch.

"Look, mom. You know how you always say that education is the key to a better job, and ultimately a better life?"

"Yeah."

"Well…" her voice quivered. She swallowed the lump in her throat. "I'm just tired of hearing you crying at night. Look. I hope you don't mind, but I filled out an application to your old school to see if you could still get in… And you did."

"What?" Kim said.

"They said that you would be able to re-enter as a junior and start where you left off."

Margie and Kim looked stunned.

"Oh my God, Kim, that sounds wonderful," Margie said. Lisa handed her mother the letter. Kim looked at it, speechless. The front in bold letters read *University Of California, Los Angeles*.

Margie was touched. "Lisa, this is a great idea," Margie said tickled.

"Mom, please," Kim said, trying to wrap her brain around it all.

"Mom, I can take a couple of years off while you go to school. Maybe you even get a master's. Then I'll go to college," Lisa said, pleading her case.

"Listen, sweetie. Great idea but not realistic," Kim said.

"Why not?" Lisa asked.

"Because, I got two jobs and three kids."

"But wait a minute, baby," Margie chimed in.

Kim quickly cut her mother off.

"Mom. It's no way in hell I could go back to school, like I'm some teenager with no responsibilities. I don't have the money, and I definitely don't have the time."

"I did your financial aid application too," Lisa added.

"Baby, you can get your degree and get a better job," Margie said, elated.

"Look, Lisa is going to Stanford like she's been planning to do for the last two years. And she's going right after graduation." Margie thought about what Kim said.

"What if I retired early and moved in with you so you can go back to school?"

"No, mom." Kim dismissed her mother's offer with a roll of the eyes.

"Why not?" Margie asked.

"Because you have your own bills."

Margie thought about it.

"Yeah, you right… But I also have a paid-off house that I can rent out."

"Mom…"

"Kim. Look, when things get better for you, then I'll move back into my house and get another job."

"But what about your retirement?"

"Hey, I'll get what I get." Kim was touched and bewildered as she played with the thought of going back to school, something that until this very minute seemed unfathomable. She looked at Lisa. Then she got up and stared at the kids playing. Her wheels were turning, thinking about her family's future as she stood there, shaking with nervous energy. A deep sigh escaped her.

"Mom, that's too much. I can't let you do that," Kim said.

"Look, baby. I know it sounds like a big sacrifice, and it is. But you're my baby. And all I'm doing is making the same sacrifice you just made for Lisa. That's all."

Lisa's eyes welled up.

"That's what being a mother's all about. Making the sacrifices that no one in the world will make. Except a mother," Margie said, with a warm smile.

Kim looked at the letter again.

"Classes started last week."

"Well, I suggest first thing Monday you go down there and start fighting to get classes," Margie replied.

Kim stood there, choked up. "I'm so tired of crying."

"You're not crying now," Margie said. Kim's emotions quickly got the best of her, as she smiled brightly through her watery eyes. Kim looked at Lisa, in awe of her sixteen-year-old daughter. She walked over to Lisa and gave her a huge hug.

"I don't know how I'm going to do this," Kim muttered.

"Me, either. You got two jobs and three kids," Margie teased. Kim and Lisa looked at Margie and they all cracked up. Margie got up and hugged them both.

Xavier and Christiahn stood staring at them, wondering what was going on. "What they so happy about," Christiahn said.

"Who knows." Xavier shrugged.

Chapter 12

THEO ENTERED WHITNEY'S SWANK BEVERLY HILLS townhome, dressed to the nines. "Nice place," Theo said, taking in the furniture and beautiful paintings. He noticed a Peter Max painting—a painting he wanted to buy for himself at one time, but it was too expensive.

"Thank you. Now that's what I call a date," Whitney said.

"So I take it you liked the play?"

"Absolutely. And the restaurant. I didn't know you could buy a steak for two hundred dollars."

"I know. I would go more, but I'm not trying to end up broke over a steak."

"Two hundred dollars, that must have been some cow… So, do you want something to drink?" Whitney offered.

"Sure."

She went to the kitchen and grabbed a pair of wine glasses.

"So what do you like, white or red?" Whitney asked from the kitchen.

"Red's fine."

Theo looked around. Her place was immaculate. He pulled out a small notepad and checked off *clean house* and *great taste*. "Not bad," Theo said to himself. He put the notepad back into his coat pocket and looked at some of her family pictures. He saw in one of them a five-year-old girl and a two-year-old boy. His expression grew sour. "Nice-looking kids," he said, tense.

"That's my niece and nephew," Whitney said from the kitchen. Theo sighed with relief.

"Oh. Cute kids."

Whitney entered the room with their wine.

"Here you go." She handed Theo his glass.

"Thank you."

"You're welcome."

"So, how long have you been living here?"

"About three years."

"You like living in Beverly Hills?"

"Ah, yeah." She smirked. They clinked their glasses and drank. When they lowered their glasses they stared at each other's lips. "So, how is Oprah in person?"

"She's cool. I mean, I didn't really get a chance to talk to her, but from what I can tell she's a genuinely nice person."

"Yeah, I heard that about her. But I heard she is no joke when it comes to her business."

"Yeah, I definitely got that impression." They continued to sip their wine.

"I think you're a cool dude, Theo."

"I think you're cool as well," Theo sighed. "And fine, and beautiful, and gorgeous, and sexy…"

"All right already. If you want some, I'll give it to you." Theo choked on his wine.

"Excuse me?"

"You heard me. If you want it?" Whitney smiled, tickled.

"Oh, I want it." He looked at her, impressed. "You don't mess around."

"I'm a lawyer, sweetie, it's not in my nature."

"I can dig it. No pun intended."

"Eww, you nasty."

They smiled and stared at each other, not saying a word. Theo downed his wine and scooted next to her, putting his arm around her. He stared at Whitney.

"You have some nice lips," Theo said.

"Thanks. So do you." Whitney stared at Theo's lips and licked her own. Theo gave a little smile and moved in for a kiss.

They kissed passionately, becoming more and more familiar with each other's lips. This went on for a few minutes, tongues dancing, as they got to know each other's rhythms. Suddenly Whitney pushed herself back. She wore a smirk, as if she was impressed and definitely curious.

"Take me to my room. Can you carry me?"

"Absolutely." Theo scooped her up and kissed her. He carried her down the hall and opened up a door and went in. It was a large closet. "My bad."

"It's okay, it'll do," Whitney said, fire in her eyes. They made out wildly, taking off each other's clothes and throwing them out of the closet.

Theo struggled with Whitney's bra as he sucked on her neck. Whitney loved it, squeezing his ass with one hand and rubbing the back of his head with the other. Theo kissed her hard on the lips, then sucked and bit her earlobe, creating the perfect tingling sensation and pain. Whitney panted, feeling her heart beat faster with each grope. Clothes fell on top of them as they made out madly. Theo finally got the bra undone, revealing her beautiful breasts. He sucked her nipples hard, squeezing her breast at the same time. She pulled him to her and kissed him, all while unbuckling his belt. She then unbuttoned his pants, reached her hand inside and squeezed. She looked up at him, surprised. He was perfect. She smiled, knowing that if he wasn't big enough there would have been a problem. At best he would have only gotten a tug to climax instead of the works.

"You like?" he said, confident.

"I like," she replied, mouth open, panting. He ripped off her panties and lay her on the floor. He pushed her legs up, positioning himself between her thighs. She locked her legs around his waist, rolled her body over on top of his. She pulled out his penis from his pants, got on top of it and rode him. Hard.

"Goddamn, girl," he said in a hurt-so-good kind of way. Clothes periodically fell on them. He stared up at Whitney as she rode him at top speed, her head back, looking up, in her own world. "Damn…"

Chapter 13

THEO ENTERED HIS HOME IN THE SAME CLOTHES HE wore the night before. He looked worn out. Like a man who just got his ass kicked. In a good way. He strolled into his office, and walked up to his oversized life chart and grabbed a marker. He wrote *Found My Wife*.

Chapter 14

THEO STOOD IN FRONT OF HIS CLASS LECTURING. ALL over the chalkboard behind him were diagrams illustrating his methods for success. He spoke passionately, using his hands for emphasis. He was in the zone, connecting with each and every one of his students.

"It's about finding your purpose and how you want to spend your life. Cause if you spend your life chasing the wrong thing, life can be long and miserable. But, if you know what you want out of life, life can be great, no matter how hard the journey to accomplishing your goals. So make the world submit to your goals. Claim it! Don't just dream about it. Make it happen. And never ever quit if it's truly what you want. So, for your homework, I want you to write down five things that you want for yourself. Then write down five things you don't want for yourself. And really, really think about it. That's your homework. Have a good weekend."

The students rose from their seats truly inspired. As Kim stood up she wiped a small tear from the corner of her eye. Another student looked at her and smiled.

"He's good, huh?" the student said.

"I had no idea," Kim replied.

"Are you okay?" the student asked, noticing Kim's emotion.

"Yeah. He just said something that hit a little too close to home, that's all." Kim smiled in appreciation of her concern, then walked up to Theo as the rest of the students cleared out.

Theo got his things together.

"Mr. Washington?" Kim said, in almost an apologetic tone.

"Yes?"

"Hi. I'm Kim Jones."

"How are you doing, Ms. Jones? You enjoying my class?"

"Yes. But technically I'm not in it."

"Oh. So you're trying to crash my course?" he said.

"Well, I was hoping I could get in."

"I'm afraid that's not likely. The class is full…"

"Oh, I didn't know. I just got in school this week." She got more emotional. "I haven't been to school in sixteen years, and I resubmitted and I got in. I wasn't gonna come back because I kind of had some personal issues, and my mother…"

"Ms. Jones, Ms. Jones… come by my office." He gave Kim a friendly wink and a smile. "I'll let you in. You're lucky— I'm in a great mood today."

Kim smiled, relieved.

"Thank you."

Kim walked into her house. Everyone was there except Lisa. Margie had her suitcases in the living room, lined up in the corner. Kim wore a smile, carrying a backpack full of books.

"Mommy's here!" Xavier and Christiahn shouted as they rushed her with hugs and kisses.

"Hey, babies," Kim said adoringly.

"So, how did it go?" Margie asked.

"It went great."

"You get all of your classes?"

"Yeah. I got a business class. Spanish class, a math class, and a class called life organization."

"Life organization?"

"Yeah, I needed an elective. This guy from TV is teaching it. He's really good.

"What's his name?"

"I don't know his first name, but his last name's Washington." The name didn't register with Margie.

"That's great, baby, I'm so happy for you."

"I am, too. I feel like I'm being given a second chance. Thanks to you." Kim hugged her mother.

"Hey, I'm just glad to see you smiling again."

Kim's smile got bigger.

"So, what do you guys want for dinner?"

"Grandma already cooked spaghetti. It was better than yours," Xavier said with a wry smile. Kim gave him a comical dirty look.

"Well, I'm glad you liked the spaghetti, Xavier." Kim said, sarcastic.

"Anyway, we're all good," Margie explained.

"Oh. Well good… I have a lot of studying to do. Mom, I'm a week behind so I have…"

"All right, go. I got this."

Kim thought for a moment.

"Lisa out?"

"Yeah. She said she told you she was going out with Kevin?"

"Yeah," Kim said, not too enthused about it. Margie laughed a little at her expression.

"Thanks, Mom." Kim kissed her mother on the cheek and went to her room. The kids' faces showed they had some adjusting to do. Especially Xavier.

"Grandma, why does she have to study?" Xavier asked.

"Yeah, why she have to study?" Christiahn echoed.

"Because, baby, she has to finish school so she can get a better job.

"I think she should get a job at the bank. They got a lot of money there," Xavier said with sincerity.

"Yes they do, baby, yes they do." Margie smiled and put her arm around Xavier.

Chapter 15

THEO SAT IN HIS LIVING ROOM GOING OVER HIS TO-do list. Whitney sat next to him working on her laptop. The phone rang. Theo got up and answered it. It was Jordan, cursing him out on the other end. Theo smiled as if it was a telemarketer.

"Thank you but no thank you… Not interested." He rolled his eyes and hung up.

"I hate when telemarketers call me, too," Whitney said, still focused on her work.

"I know. It's the worst."

"Oh, I think I might be able to help your friend," Whitney said, looking up from her computer.

"What?" Theo asked, not knowing what she was talking about.

"Your cousin. I think I might be able to get him a job at my firm."

"Who, Sam?"

"You have any other unemployed cousins? But yeah. You said he was in maintenance, right?"

"Yeah."

"He's reliable? Cause I don't want to vouch for him if he's a flake."

"Yeah, Sam is extremely dependable. He's like my big brother."

"Then tell him to come to my office on Monday."

"I will thanks." Theo looked at her, impressed. He jotted down on his note pad *thoughtful*. The doorbell rang. "Ah hell, that's my manager, David. Prepare yourself."

"Do you want me to leave so you can talk business?"

"No, no, it's fine." Theo answered the door.

David Gonzales, a Latino in his early forties, strolled in wearing a tailor-made suit with a button-down shirt open at the neck. He wore a gold watch and a diamond pinky ring. He was Mr. Personality.

"How's it going, brother?" David asked, letting out a big sigh as though he just got off work.

They hugged and walked through the foyer to the living room.

"Good. How was your flight?"

"All right I guess. There was a whining-ass baby in first class that kept me up. That's got to be against the law."

"Well, babies gotta fly, too."

"Not in first class they don't… oh my goodness," David said, totally caught off guard by Whitney, leaving his mouth wide open.

Whitney got up from the couch and put her laptop on the coffee table preparing to meet David. Theo rolled his eyes, knowing how David was.

"David, this is my friend Whitney."

"Very nice to meet you," David said, impressed. He shook Whitney's hand, then kissed it.

"Nice to meet you as well," she replied. David gave Theo a look, like *How did you pull this off?* David continued to hold Whitney's hand, looking her over wearing a perverted smile. Theo separated them.

"Hands off," Theo said to David with a smirk.

"Not bad," David said under his breath to Theo, as if Whitney could not hear him. She blushed and smiled, charmed by him.

"Behave," Theo said.

"I'm just saying."

"So you're the man behind the man," Whitney said wearing a smile.

"In the flesh. Yeah, I give him all his great ideas."

"In your dreams. Basically he books my flights."

"Anyway. I'm David Gonzales. Manager extraordinaire."

"Are you done trying to impress?" Theo asked.

"No. I mean yes. Anyway…" Under his breath to Theo. "Here's your plane ticket." Whitney chuckled. "We also have a couple of dates that I just added to your schedule."

"All right."

"Like I said, we got to hit it hard."

"I know, I know. Hit it hard. You say that all the time."

"I know I do. And what do we do all the time?"

"Hit it hard," Theo said with a knowing smile.

"Exactly. So anyway, Whitney. Do you have a sister that looks just like you, or maybe a cousin, cousin by marriage even?" Whitney blushed and laughed again.

"No, not that I can think of."

"Well, if you think of any, you give me a call immediately. Because you are stunning." Whitney laughed. David whipped out his card like a gunslinger drawing his Colt 45 and handed it to her.

"Thank you."

"Are you done?" Theo asked.

"No. Personally, I think you're too good looking for Theo. But that's a whole other conversation."

"Are you trying to get thrown out of my house?"

"Hey, I'm just playing." He looked at Whitney. "No I'm not." He looked at Theo. "You know I am." He looked back at Whitney. "No I'm not." He looked back at Theo. "So did Sam get his job back?" Theo looked at him, shaking his head. Whitney thought David was funny and was flattered by him.

Chapter 16

KIM AND MARGIE SAT ON THE FRONT PORCH reading while the kids played. Kim read one of her schoolbooks. Margie read the newspaper.

"God, mom. I feel like my brain is about to explode. I hope I didn't overdo it by taking a full load."

"You'll be fine," Margie replied.

"I miss spending time with the kids already."

"Don't worry, baby, it'll all be worth it. You'll see."

"I hope so."

"Did your financial aid go through?"

"Yeah, Lisa took care of it."

"Good." The two looked at the kids playing.

"They're growing so fast."

"That's the way life is. If you're not paying attention, it will just pass you right on by." Christiahn approached Kim.

"Mom, do my hair?"

"No, baby. I have to study."

"Okay," Christiahn said, about to go back to play with Xavier and Lisa.

"Come here, Christiahn, I'll do it," Margie said. Christiahn instantly smiled and walked over to Margie. Kim felt bad. "Remember what I told you about what your mother's doing?"

"School?" Christiahn said, as she positioned herself between Margie's legs.

"That's right."

Margie went to work on her hair.

Kim stared at Christiahn, then continued to study. She thought about her kids and her late husband. She thought about the odds of losing her soulmate at such a young age. They planned to spend the rest of their lives together. She said to herself, *What the hell happened?* Was this God's way of testing her or did this terrible incident in her life have nothing to do with God?

It was just life itself. And now she wanted to make the best of this situation. This thing called *life*. A thing of surprise and heartbreak. A thing of joy and happiness. She said to herself, *I'm going to take full advantage of this opportunity.* With so much on the line, Kim had to bring her A-Game and make this school thing work, no matter what.

With the exception of Lisa, the whole family sat in a circle that night.

"Look, I just wanted to talk to you guys about what mommy's trying to do. I know I told you guys already, but I just want to be clear," Kim said in a loving tone, feeling the guilt because of the tough journey she knew lay ahead.

"Mom, we understand," Xavier chimed in.

"Yeah, I know, but I just want you guys to know that I am doing this for our family."

"We understand, mom. You're doing it to get a better job," Xavier said matter-of-factly like he would rather be somewhere else. Christiahn stared at Xavier.

"Leave mommy alone," Christiahn said, glaring at Xavier.

"Shut up, Christiahn, you too young to know what's going on," Xavier responded with his own evil eye.

"You shut up," Christiahn shot back.

"Will you guys both be quiet? Damn!" Kim said, trying to control her stress.

"See, mom's going to snap again," Xavier said. They looked at each other, then Kim busted out laughing. They all joined in.

"I just want to say two years are going to go by so fast. So we gotta be tough. And it's going to take just as much adjusting on my part."

"What's adjusting mean?" Xavier asked.

"Getting used to… It's just so hard without your father being here."

"Is daddy coming back?" Christiahn asked earnestly. This broke Kim and Margie's heart. Xavier's too. His eyes brimmed with tears.

"No, baby, he's not. But I'm here. And we have your grandma. And your father is here," Kim said, pointing to Christiahn's heart. "I just love you guys so much. And I wish I could be with you guys all the time."

"You sure about that?" Margie asked. They both gave a little smile. The kids smiled with a scowl, getting the joke.

"Okay, maybe not all the time. Mommies need a break, too. Because you guys are not easy."

"We're not?" Christiahn asked with puppy dog eyes.

"No, baby, you're not," Kim said, amused. "But I love you so much it doesn't matter. So what we are doing is making a sacrifice right now. So that we don't have to struggle. Because Daddy's not here to help us." The kids looked at each other as if they got it. "That's why I have to make every moment count.

Although this is going to be a tough two years, we are going to get through it."

"I know we will, mom. I'll do whatever I can to help," Xavier said.

"Me, too," Christiahn added, trying to outdo Xavier.

"Well, this is what family is all about," Margie said.

"Absolutely. So just remember, you guys, we are a family, and this is going to be a team effort, okay?"

"Okay, mom," the kids said in unison.

Margie and Kim looked at each other, becoming a little emotional.

"Group hug," Kim said. The kids rushed her with hugs.

"Group hug," Christiahn repeated.

Suddenly, Lisa barged into the house, crying, stomping through the living room headed straight for her room. Lisa slammed her bedroom door shut. They all wondered what was wrong.

Chapter 17

WHITNEY PREPARED DINNER FOR THEO AT HER home, while soft music played in the background.

"Sam's happy," Theo said.

"He told you he got it?"

"Yeah. Thank you for that. My man's got a daughter going to college. So he really can't afford to be out of work."

"Glad I could help." She sat down and they got ready to eat.

"The food looks great."

"One thing my mom taught us was how to cook." They smiled and bowed their heads for a quick beat, then started to eat.

"Wow," he said as he chewed his food.

"You like?" she asked, confident.

"I like," he said, almost blushing, the food was so good. She leaned over and gave Theo a kiss. "That was nice," He said with a charmed, smile.

"I know it was," she said, not missing a beat.

"Kind of cocky, aren't you?"

"You want another one don't you?" she said with a confident smile.

"Actually, this cornbread is kind of taking precedence right now." She playfully threw a carrot at him. "I'm just saying, the cornbread's good." They laughed. He took another big bite out of his cornbread, then got up and took her hand. They began to slow dance. Their bodies close, letting their heartbeats provide the rhythm. Suddenly Whitney's eyes turned sorrowful.

"I have to tell you something."

"What?" Theo replied. Her sad eyes worried him.

"You might not like it."

"I'm a big boy. I can handle it."

"I went out with my old boyfriend a couple of days ago." Theo stopped dancing.

"Is that right?"

"Yeah."

"So what happened?" Whitney's eyes lowered with guilt. "Wow," Theo said taking a step back.

"Look, I just wanted to be straight up with you. I like you and I really want this to work."

"Well then, why?"

"He called me out of the blue, telling me he had made a huge mistake, and I just wanted to be sure. I mean, he was my boyfriend for three years."

Theo stared at her with a blank expression. He tried to mask his pain by making his eyes smile again, but Whitney could see he was hurt.

"Why are you telling me this?"

"Because I didn't want to keep any secrets from you. I don't do the lying thing. Plus, I felt like you deserved to know."

"Well, hey, we're not married. Hell, we just met. It's all good." He reached for his jacket but she stopped him.

"Look, don't do that. I didn't mean to hurt you. I just wanted to be truthful with you." They stared at each other. Theo took a moment before he spoke.

"So, are you sure?" he asked, swallowing the lump of disdain in his throat.

"Yes. I am." She gave him a soft kiss on the lips. He didn't kiss her back. "C'mon, now. Don't be like that. I told you, I'm sure." She kissed him again, until he finally gave in and kissed her back.

The next night Theo was going over papers in his office at the University while eating a chicken dinner. His computer *beeped*. It was an email from David with his flight and hotel confirmation for Atlanta. He looked at his watch and took two final bites of his corn on the cob.

Theo strolled through the UCLA parking lot, his attaché case in hand. It was getting dark and the campus lights were starting to come on. As he walked, he thought about his next book. He knew the pressure was on—he had to hit a home run with this one. Thanks to his bitter ex-girlfriend Jordan, it had to be an undeniable success. But what, he wondered. He had covered so much in all of his previous books. He knew this one had to be something fresh. Something new. The kind of work that defines a period in time. Like Alex Haley's book *Roots*. Or even the *Beatles* music. Or *Motown*.

As he strolled through the campus parking lot in deep thought, he saw Kim, looking under the hood of her tattered Buick. He did a double-take, then walked over to see if he could be of any help.

She had her head under the hood when he walked up behind her. "Having problems?"

"Yeah, I don't know what it is," Kim said, unaware that she was speaking to Theo.

"Here, let me take a look," Theo said.

She lifted her head from under the hood.

"Mr. Washington!"

"Kim, right?"

"Yeah."

"Let me see what's going on in here."

"I thought it was the battery."

"What happened?"

"I don't know. It just cut off on me."

"So, it started up first?"

"Yeah. It started up, then cut off."

"Eww."

"What?"

He checked the cables, making sure that nothing was loose.

"That doesn't seem like just the battery... All your wires are connected. Wait a minute, this one's kind of loose." He pushed the cable in the socket, then pulled his head out from under the hood. "All right, try it now."

"Well back up; I don't want it to explode in your face."

Theo smiled.

"I'll be all right. Now give it a try." He thought about it again, then backed up just to be safe. She tried to start it, but nothing happened. "Did you pump the gas when it first cut off?"

"Yeah."

"A lot?"

"Yeah," she said, knowing she shouldn't have.

"I think you flooded it," Theo said, shaking his head.

"Damn! Oops, I'm sorry."

"Ay, I'm your professor, not your priest."

Kim just smiled, shaking her head at her predicament.

"Do you have a cell phone? My cell battery's dead, too."
They smiled, amused at the irony of the situation.

"Sure." He went to his hip for his cell, but it wasn't there.
He remembered it was in his attaché case.

"Yeah, my battery runs out if I use it for more than five
minutes."

He pulled his cell out of his bag.

"I'll call Triple A."

"No, I'm gonna call my mom. I got some Triple A
issues."

"You can use my card."

"No. I'll just call for a ride."

"Look, I don't want to just leave you out here."

"No, it's okay. I'll be fine. I have a friend who fixes cars.
We'll get it running tomorrow."

"Are you sure?" Theo asked.

"Yeah."

"Okay. It probably is just flooded."

"So… do you think I can use your cell to call my mom?"

"Oh yeah, here." He was about to hand it to her but then stopped. "Look. How about I just take you home so you don't have to be out here in the dark."

She thought about it for a moment, knowing that her mom would have to get the kids dressed, put them all in the mini-van, and drive way down there.

"Nah, I don't want to inconvenience you…"

"It's not a problem."

"You sure you don't mind?" she asked.

"Yeah, I'm sure. C'mon."

"Okay, if you're sure you don't mind?"

"It's not a problem." Theo smiled and closed the hood.

Kim looked uncomfortable in his car. "Are you okay?" Theo asked, as he drove.

"Yeah, I'm fine." Kim smiled. "Oh, and thanks again for the ride."

"No problem… So, Kim, what made you decide to go back to school after sixteen years?"

"Get a better job and make more money. I'm afraid it's just that simple."

"That sounds like a good reason to me. People say money doesn't buy happiness, and they're right. But having it means that's just one less thing to worry about." Kim admired the car's beautiful black and tan interior, and it's new car smell.

"I know that's the truth. You know, when you're younger, it seems like you have forever to do the things you want to do in life. Next thing you know, you're thirty-six and haven't accomplished any of the things you thought you would of."

"That's because you have to seize the moment. And it looks like that's what you're doing now. And that's all that matters. Whether you're thirty-six or seventy-six."

"That's easy for you to say. How old are you?"

"Thirty-two. Hey, I got lucky. I know that. But even if I didn't have the career I have, I'd still be doing the same thing. Writing books, speaking to people, inspiring. I just wouldn't be on Oprah and CNN." They continued to ride. "You'll get there," Theo said with a sense of certainty.

"I'm trying."

"People make life more complicated than it has to be... Life is very simple. You make a plan and you don't deviate from that plan," Theo said, as if it was the easiest thing to do.

"Yeah, but sometimes life throws you a curveball."

"Then you adapt and work with that curveball you've been thrown."

"Sometimes that's easier said than done."

"Not if you have a plan."

"But sometimes it depends on how big that curveball is," Kim said, as she thought about her own curveball.

Theo answered her without missing a beat, schooling her on the rules of life.

"You'd be surprised what God has put in us to handle even those big curveballs."

As they drove through an intersection, a car ran a red light. Theo slammed on the brakes, stopping almost instantly. They both screamed, just missing the car. Theo screamed with a higher pitch than Kim. The two of them panted, catching their breath, eyes wide in a state of shock. They looked down, realizing they were squeezing each other's hands. They let go with a strong sigh and remained in the intersection, gathering themselves.

"Your brakes are the shit!" Kim said, still shook. Theo nodded *yes*, amused but traumatized. He punched it through the intersection.

As Theo continued to drive Kim home, his navigational system told him to *make a right turn*. As he turned, he smiled about his near fatal brush with death and Kim's remark about his brakes being *the shit*.

Kim did a double-take at the big piece of corn on the side of his front teeth. She tightened her lips, trying not to laugh.

"Think of it this way, Kim. If you want to be something, all you have to do is not quit. That's it. That's the whole secret to life right there. Not to quit."

She thought about it.

"That makes sense. You know, I looked you up on the Internet."

Theo laughed.

"What's up with the internet? It seems like everyone goes there after they meet me."

"Well, people want to know who they're dealing with. You could be a madman."

"I guess." They each gave a little laugh.

"Speaking of crazy people, have you ever heard of a woman named Jordan Yikes?" Theo smiled, amused.

"Yeah, I have," Theo replied.

"Cause she has it out for you. Yikes." Kim laughed at her own corny joke.

"She's my ex. And she's kind of crazy."

"You think?" Kim said knowingly. They laughed. Theo liked her sense of humor. "But seriously, the things you say. You speak the truth, Mr. Washington, and one thing my mom always says. If you're not telling the truth, you're just wasting your breath."

"Ooh, that's a good one. I'm gonna steal that one and put it in my next book." He chuckled and pulled up at a stop sign. He pulled out a notepad and wrote it down real fast. "Your mother sounds like a wise woman."

"She is. That's my house on the left. The blue one." Theo turned into the driveway. "Well, thanks again for the ride."

"No problem."

"I hope I didn't take you too far out of your way."

"Hey, it was my pleasure. Plus, I got a quote out of it."

She smiled, thankful.

"So, I'll see you in class." Theo said with a smile. The corn had moved onto his front teeth. She smiled, trying her best not to laugh.

"See you there. Oh, and you got something in your teeth." She hopped out of the car.

He quickly looked in the rearview mirror.

"Bye, Mr. Washington." She closed the door and headed to the house.

He spotted the big piece of corn on his front teeth. He quickly wiped it away, embarrassed. He watched Kim as she headed to her house, carrying her coat. He gave a little laugh, then tilted his head to the side, noticing she had a great big ass.

The Five Steps of Mr. Washington

"Goddamn…"

Chapter 18

KIM AND LISA WERE IN THE GROCERY MARKET shopping. Lisa's hair was wrapped in a scarf, and she was wearing all black as if she was in mourning. Kim looked her up and down as she picked fruit. "Lisa, are you ready to talk about it?"

"Talk about what?"

"The reason you've been locked in your room for the past week."

"I don't wanna talk about it."

"Why not?" Kim asked.

"Because."

"Girl, you better tell me what the hell is going on?"

Lisa thought about it, knowing her mother would never let up. "Okay, I'm sure you already know it's about Kevin," Lisa said.

Kim smirked.

"What happened?" Kim asked, a bad taste in her mouth.

"We broke up."

Margie's frown turned into a huge smile.

"Oh, that's terrible."

"See, mom, that's why I didn't want to talk to you about it. Because you think you know him, but you don't."

"Honey, I just want you to be happy, that's all."

"Well, I'm not. I'm freakin' pissed and depressed."

"It doesn't help when you're holding all that anger inside. You have to talk about it."

"Mom, don't try to help."

"What happened?"

"He was cheating with some other girl."

"How'd you find out?"

"One of my friends saw them together at the mall."

"Did he admit to it?"

"He didn't have to. She took a picture of him with her phone."

"Well, maybe they were just friends?"

"They were in the Victoria Secret store, holding hands."

"Hmm. He was cheating all right. Did you tell him you had a picture of him and the girl?"

"I figured, why bother? I'm sure he would of came up with some bullshit."

"Lisa, do you have to say bullshit?"

Lisa gave her mother an *Are you kidding me* look.

"Okay, my bad. You were at 'bullshit'."

"Anyway, it is what it is."

"I'm sorry, honey. You know I wasn't the biggest fan of that boy, but I know how it is to have your heartbroken."

"My heart's not broken. I'm just mad as hell. The girl isn't even that cute."

"They never are."

"Men suck."

"Not all men. Your dad was a great man. He was kind and generous. He loved me so much. He was my best friend."

"Well that's the thing, Kevin would tell me how much he loved me all of the time, and how he wanted us to be together forever. He even took me to his church. Which he goes every Sunday."

Kim had to roll her eyes to that one.

"It doesn't matter what a man says, it matters what a man does. How he treats you. How he conveys his love. Words don't mean anything if the action isn't behind it. Hell, that's the problem I have with religion. All these people talking about God and how much they love him, but then they'll do their fellow man or woman dirty in a second."

"Mom, don't go into the religion thing. I'm sorry I even mentioned it."

"I'm just saying, him going to church means nothing if he acts an ass all the time. Remember his Christian ass left you at the beach when you guys had that big fight. Who does that? I had to leave my job to pick you up."

"I know, mom. You never let me forget."

"People think being a Christian is about reciting chapters and verses. And it's not. It's about how you treat people. That's what's wrong with all religion. Everyone's judging everybody, telling people who's going to hell and who's not and how they should be living. It's so stupid. Jeez, just treat people how you want to be treated."

"Mom. This conversation is supposed to be about me," Lisa said.

"You know, your grandmother got saved some years ago and damn near lost her mind. She went to some church that was saying that the only way to heaven is through their church.

"Huh?"

"You heard me. All of the other churches were going to hell because they didn't believe in God their way. Like out of all of the churches around the world, this church, that had only been around for five years, run by a thirty-year-old pastor, had all the answers."

"Amen to that, mom," Lisa said with a chuckle, amused by the rant.

Kim gave Lisa a look to take her words to heart. She continued to vent. "I love Jesus just like the next person, but at the end of the day it's all based on faith. So since that is the case, people just need to shut the hell up when it comes to telling someone else how to live their life, especially if they're not hurting anyone. And it's always the people who done the most shit in their life that want to judge. You know what they say, you can stand in a garage but that doesn't make you a car."

"Huh!" Lisa laughed.

"Think about it."

Lisa's face showed it registered.

"Oh, that's deep."

"And don't get me started on the pastors. One of them has the nerve to name himself after money. What is that? Jesus didn't call himself *Check Book*. He was all about loving and helping people."

"I think you should become a pastor."

"I should. Call myself Dollar-Fifty. And pay off some of these bills." They laughed. "I'm just saying, I'm so disappointed in these crooked-ass pastors nowadays. I know they're not all bad. I know there some awesome pastors out there. But a lot of them aren't right. Most of them just want to be celebrities and treated like stars. They should just call themselves entrepreneurs slash motivational speakers, not pastors. Then I wouldn't have a problem with it. There's nothing wrong with getting rich. But using the Lord to guilt broke people into giving their light bill money so they can have these extravagant lifestyles. Shooed! Tell people to tithe with their time. Or tithe in other ways. We all know someone who could use a knock on the door, and say, hey, I heard you just got a divorce, or your husband died, and I just wanted to bless you. Tell people to tithe like that sometime... Did I tell you that your grandmother refinanced her home 'cause the church needed a new sound system? She gave them twenty-five thousand dollars. I mean, how many speakers do a place need? Now, six months later, your dad and I are broke cause he lost his job. I mean, we had nothing. So she asked her pastor if the church could help us out. You know what the pastor said?"

"What?" Lisa asked.

"He said that God was testing us. And he didn't want to mess with the Lord's test... I'm just tired of people taking advantage of others. Especially when life is already whupping their ass. It's a dog-eat-dog world, and if people can take advantage of other people, whether it be in church or businesses, most of the time they will. That's why we don't have no damn health insurance, cause it's a really rich person who owns the company I work for, who wants to be even richer. So screw the people who work for them." Lisa stared at her mother, who looked beat by life. "And that's why I want you go to Stanford.

Forget all about that little big-head boy. And develop you a skill that will make your employers have to respect and value you, and pay you your worth. Or, even better, start your own business."

Lisa rubbed her mother's back, thinking about her words and the truth in them.

"Mom… you need Jesus." Kim looked at Lisa strangely, then busted out laughing.

"I know. I'm trying."

They laughed, as they continued to shop.

Chapter 19

PEOPLE HUSTLED IN AND OUT OF A HIGH-RISE ON Wilshire Boulevard, going on with their workday.

Theo strolled through the lobby looking dapper as usual. He got on the elevator, joining two other men already on it. Theo went to press the number twelve button, but it was already lit.

"I'm just going to keep my head down and do my job," one man said.

"I hear you. That's all you can do," the other man added.

"It just pisses me off. Everyone knows she takes credit when it's her idea. But when it's my idea or your idea? She snaps into, *Oh it was a team effort. The team, the team.*"

"Yep. She's not even that talented. I mean everyone knows that Brad should be running the department, not her."

"And she knows it, too."

"Man, I just want to say it to her face so bad. Whitney Mansfield. I know you're not as talented as me, and you know you're not as talented as me, so please, please, please, stop being a bitch to everyone around you who could do your job better than you."

Theo gave the men a quick glance. "And learn how to talk to people. You don't have to be a bitch to your assistants and everyone below you just because you can," the other man added.

Ding. The elevator doors slid open. Theo stepped out with the two men bothered a little by their conversation. He walked to the reception desk.

"Hello. Theo Washington here to see Ms. Whitney Mansfield."

The two men walked by, hearing him.

"Fuck me," one of them said to the other in passing. Theo shrugged as they walked by.

"Sure, one moment," the receptionist said with a courteous smile.

"Thank you."

She patched through to Whitney.

"Ms. Mansfield, there is a Mr. Theo Washington here..." She looked up at Theo. "She'll be out in a moment." Theo took a seat in the waiting area.

Whitney came out, beaming. "Oh my God, I thought you weren't getting back from Atlanta until tomorrow."

"I thought I'd surprise you…"

"Well, come on in." She motioned toward her office. They strolled inside and closed the door. She kissed him on the lips. "So, Mr. Washington, what brings you by?"

"I thought I would take you out to get some lunch."

"I missed you," Whitney said, looking at him adoringly.

"I was only gone three days."

"Three days too many." She kissed him again, wearing a big smile.

"Is that right?"

"That's right. Let me get my purse." She grabbed her purse and keys while Theo enjoyed the view of the city from Whitney's office.

"So, how's Sam doing?" Theo asked, hoping for the best.

"As far as I know, they love him."

"Good."

"Look, I wanna get a room at the *W* down the street for a quickie, work up an appetite, and then get something to eat. Is that okay?"

Theo smiled, amused by her candor.

"That's very okay."

Theo gulped his water like he was dehydrated, while Whitney ate like a refugee. They dined in the restaurant at the *W* amongst a large crowd.

"I love food after sex," Whitney said with a mouthful of food. Theo finished his glass of water and put it down next to two other empty glasses. He looked at Whitney fascinated, as she shoveled food in her mouth.

"You were something else. You know that?" Theo said.

"I know. You just got to get in shape, that's all. Especially if you wanna hang with me."

Theo smirked.

"Anyway. I've been thinking, maybe we should go on a vacation when school is out for me."

"I think that's a great idea."

"Yeah, maybe Jamaica or Hawaii. What do you think?"

"I've been to both; I could go to either one," she replied.

"In that case, why don't we go to Australia? You been there?"

"No."

"Well, let's go there?"

"Sounds good to me. But I must tell you, I'm not for all that sightseeing. I like to go to a couple of places, have lots of sex in the hotel room, and I'm good."

"Hey, I'm down with a whole bunch of sex in the hotel room, too. But you just can't go to Australia and not see the sites."

"And why not?"

"Because you just can't. You have to plan your trip so you can see everything they have to offer. Okay, look at it this way. You've been to Rome, right?"

"Yeah."

"It's like going there and not having seen the Sistine Chapel."

"Actually, I didn't make it there," she said matter-of-factly.

Theo was stunned.

"What do you mean, you didn't make it there?"

"I didn't make it."

"You've got to be kidding me."

"No. But I could tell you about some really great restaurants out there."

"You are kidding me?"

"Hey, I'm gonna see it eventually."

"Wow…" Theo said, bewildered.

"Like I said. I don't like going on vacation and burning myself out trying to see everything. I go to relax. Hence the word vacation."

Theo looked at her like he still couldn't get over it.

"But it's the Sistine Chapel. Michelangelo, man."

"Well, if it makes you feel any better, I'll look at it tonight on the Internet."

Theo was appalled.

She continued to eat. She was amused. "Okay, next time I get to Rome, I'll go. Okay?"

"Hey, it's all good. Maybe seeing some of the greatest artwork ever done in the whole wide world is not your thing."

"Will you just shut up and give me some sugar?" Theo smiled and leaned in to give her a kiss.

"No, I mean the sugar for my iced tea."

He passed her the sugar with a smirk, outdone with the conversation. She continued to eat. She looked at his frustrated expression and gave a smile, hoping he would lighten up. He gave her a hint of a smile back.

"Boy, you can really eat."

"I know. My mom always says, *good thing you workout. Cause if you didn't, you'd be big as a house*."

"I guess so," Theo said staring at her while she poured sugar into her iced tea. "Guess what?"

"What?"

"I just started my new book." He showed the excitement in his eyes, trying his best to convey the importance of what he was saying. "It hit me in Atlanta and, man, I think this book is gonna be, without a doubt, my best one."

"Oh, that's great," Whitney said more involved with her meal than what he was talking about. She continued to eat. Theo sat there waiting for her to ask what the book was about. She never did.

Chapter 20

THEO STOOD IN FRONT OF HIS CLASS LECTURING. HE was passionate as usual.

"So when you ask yourself, what do you want to become, you also have to think about the lifestyle you want. Do you want to be a family man or woman or do you just want to make a lot of money? Or maybe you just want to save the world. Hell, I'd like to be a rock star. But would I want the lifestyle of one?"

"Shit, yeah!" one of the male students yelled out. Everyone laughed. Theo chuckled, letting the laughs subside before responding.

"Okay, I hear you. You might want to travel around the world, party every night, have sex with different women… or men," Theo said to the male student who's smile quickly turned into a frown. Students laughed. "Money. People wanting to take your pictures and ask for your autograph everywhere you go… But then there's no privacy. Everyone's constantly staring at you. If you pick your nose, hell, it might end up in a magazine. Who knows? You might even get some death threats here and there because some crazy person thinks you were talking about them in one of your songs. And everyone is going to want to sue you… Also, night after night on tour buses, riding down dark roads, nine months out of the year away from your family. So you can forget about getting that father or mother of the year award… So you have to ask yourself. Is that what you want? You have to think about the lifestyle. If you don't like to answer to anyone, you might want to be an entrepreneur and own your own business. If you are a people person, maybe you might want to be an event planner or publicist. Homebody; maybe a writer. Do you get where I'm going? So, I want you all to write a five-page paper on the lifestyle you want. Not the career. But the lifestyle. All right… see you next week."

The students got up to leave. Theo saw Kim getting her things together. "Kim. Could I speak to you for a moment?"

Kim looked a little surprised and walked over to him.

"So, how's the car?"

"It started up no problem," Kim said.

"Good. I figured it would."

"But seriously, thanks again. It would have taken forever for my mom to pick me up."

"Well, the pleasure was all mine. Hey, when my car breaks down you can return the favor."

"Yeah, right. I don't think your car is going to be breaking down anytime soon." They both gave a laugh, flirting a little. "Bye, Mr. Washington…"

"Theo."

"Okay. Theo. Oh by the way, I left you something at your office." She waved, smiling as she walked off. He smiled back, curious.

Theo got his papers together and walked out of the classroom down to his office. When he got inside, he saw two pieces of corn on the cob on a plate, in cling wrap. There was a box of toothpicks next to it. He cracked up.

Chapter 21

THEO, DAVID, AND SAM CHILLED OUT IN FRONT OF Starbucks.

"I'm telling you, Sam, I found you a sweet girl. She's nice, thoughtful…. Big booty." They laughed.

"All right, hook it up. What's her name?"

"Kim… Kim Jones."

Theo had his notepad out, looking over his notes.

Whitney's flaws 1. No culture 2. Eat too much. 3. Self absorbed. Whitney's virtues 1. Thoughtful. 2. Sexy. 3. Fun.

David looked at the notepad. "What's that? Ideas for the new book?" he asked, eager.

"Nope," Theo said with a smirk.

"Yes it is. C'mon, Theo, tell me about this new book!"

"Not gonna do it. I'm trying something different this time."

"But I'm your fucking manager."

"Exactly. And I don't want you telling me that I should do it this way or do it that way in order to sell more books."

"Did he tell you what the book is about?" David asked Sam.

"Of course," Sam said, matter-of-factly.

"That ain't right. Is Sam gonna get you on CNN?"

"I don't know, maybe he will," Theo said.

"You know, I do know one of the maintenance guys over there," Sam said, amused.

"See, he knows one of the maintenance guys," Theo said with a smile.

"Get the fuck outta here," David said, shaking his head in frustration.

"See. You got to stop underestimating people," Theo said.

"Theo, you don't deserve me." Theo and Sam laughed.

"Ease up, David. You know we're just playing with you," Theo said with a wry smile.

"Ha ha, very funny. So, you're gonna tell me?"

Theo thought about it for a moment.

"No," he said with a laugh behind it.

"Did you really tell Sam?"

Sam smiled, chuckling.

"Yes," Theo said.

"You guys are full of shit. I'm going to get some more coffee." David got up in a huff. Theo and Sam laughed as David saw a beautiful woman and redirected himself toward her.

"You gotta love him," Theo said.

"He's a character, all right," Sam added.

"So, things are going good over there at the new job?"

"So far so good," Sam replied.

"Cool,"

They both exhaled, taking in their environment.

"So what is it you wanted to ask me?" Theo said.

"Look, man, I don't know if I'm overstepping my boundaries or not."

Theo looked on, intrigued.

"What is it?"

"I'm only bringing this up because I know how much of a tight ass you are when it comes to just about everything you do. Including women. And since you're talking about making someone Mrs. Washington, and I'm sure that's what you're working on over there. And you probably got some kind of schematic, five-point plan to marrying her…"

"Spit it out."

"Well, she just don't seem like your type, that's all."

"What do you mean not my type?"

"Man, that girl is evil as hell."

"Are we talking about the same woman?"

"Hell yeah."

"Look, the woman I know is sweet, kind, and affectionate. Hell, she even got your ass a job," Theo said, baffled.

"I know. And trust me, man, I'm grateful. But…"

"But what?"

"Man, she is mean as hell," Sam said, laughing. "I've heard her cussin' people out left and right. She had one guy crying like a baby. Imagine that, a grown-ass man crying like a damn infant… And she's always gossiping. She'll tell a person's business at the drop of a dime."

"How do you know all this?"

"Because I'm the maintenance man, and we get the scoop on everything."

"Is that right?"

"That's right. People get to a certain level and trust me. If you're cleaning, you become invisible."

"Look, she's an attorney and you have to be a little cutthroat in that field to get to the top. It's hella competitive."

"Okay. I just wanted to pull your coat to it, that's all."

"It's pulled," Theo said, a little irritated.

"By the way, I heard from the ladies in the mail room that you are an excellent lay." Sam held up his coffee cup with a smile. "That little ear thing you do." Sam laughed. Theo's face dropped.

Chapter 22

THEO PULLED UP AT HIS HOUSE—SURPRISED WHEN he saw Coco sitting on the front porch. He was concerned because he didn't invite her, nor did he know how she knew where he lived.

He got out of the car and approached her. "Hey, what's up, sweetie?"

"Sorry for dropping by like this. I'm kind of going through a personal crisis."

"How did you find my house?"

"Google."

"Oh." Theo nodded, thinking *That damn, Google.* "Everything okay?"

"Yeah, I just needed to talk, and you know I don't know anyone out here," she said, looking stressed out.

"Do you want to come in?"

"No, I just need some advice. And this is your field of expertise." Theo sat down beside her.

"What's up?" Theo asked.

Coco took a moment, then let it out.

"What do you think about me?"

"Huh?

"You heard me. What do you think about me?" she asked, looking into his eyes.

"I think you're a really sweet person."

"Really?"

"Yeah."

"Well, what would you think if I slept with two clients?"

"I would think that's what she does." He gave her a look that said *Is this a trick question?*

"I know that's the business I'm in. But I don't sleep with two guys at once."

"Oh."

"I mean this is something I said I would never do. I don't do drugs, I don't do orgies, and I don't sleep with girls cause I'm not a lesbian."

"It sounds like you've given this a lot of thought."

"Yeah, but two guys want to offer me fifteen thousand dollars."

"Oh."

"I mean, where do I draw the line?"

"Nobody can tell you where that line is but you. You have to decide that."

"I know, but it's fifteen thousand dollars. Which would get me that much closer to getting my own salon. And out of this business forever."

"Or closer to you losing your mind."

She's taken aback by his words.

"What do you mean?" she asked, perplexed.

"You can't put a price on your sanity, sweetie. That's yours, and you shouldn't let no one mess with that, no matter what the price. Now if you're okay with it, and it doesn't bother you to sleep with two men, then who am I or anyone to judge? It's your life. But, if it's something that you think you'll lose, that you won't be able to recover from, then don't do it. You're smart. You know what the right answer is."

"You think I'm smart?" Coco asked, looking into his eyes.

"Yes, I do."

Coco smiled at the thought of someone thinking she was smart.

"You just don't want to compromise yourself. Lord knows, I've done some things that I'm not proud of. Hell, I know you want to get your money to start this beauty salon, but, sweetie, you want to be proud at how you accomplish your goals in life."

She stared at him for a long moment.

"You think I'm a ho, don't you?" she said with a tinge of sarcasm. "And no, it's not a trick question." They both laughed.

"Of course I don't think you're a ho. If you're a ho, I guess I'm a ho, too. Let me tell you something. And I've never told anyone this before. But back when I just got out of college, I got a job at a radio station, and my boss was a straight-up cougar. And she was on me. Slapping my ass all of the time and I didn't want to say anything 'cause I felt like this was a great opportunity. And within three months of being there, a job opened up as a program director and, hell, I wasn't qualified for it. I barely had any experience. But one night, when I was working late at the station and it was just the two of us, she offered me the job if I'd sleep with her."

Coco stared at him, amazed that he would tell her something like this.

"So what did you do?"

"Fucked the hell out of her…"

Coco almost choked, before busting out laughing. They continued to laugh hard and long.

"So I guess we just… a couple of ho's," Theo said.

"I guess so."

They stopped laughing, catching their breath.

"At the end of the day, we all do shit that we're not proud of, things that we wanna take back. But the truth is, sometimes doing the wrong thing can make us grow in a way, that doing the right thing could have never done for us. But you still want to do the right thing. Because it's right. And doing the wrong thing is stupid. I'm starting to confuse myself now."

They laughed. He figured he'd make sense of it later and put it in his new book.

"No, I get what you're saying," she said, wearing a pretty smile. "It make sense."

"You good, shorty?" he said, making a poor attempt to be hip.

She laughed.

"I'm good, boo. And thanks for calling me smart."

They both took in the quiet of Theo's well-to-do neighborhood, watching a middle-aged woman across the street water her grass without a care in the world.

Coco smiled, then kissed Theo on the cheek.

Chapter 23

KIM SAT ON THE SOFA STUDYING HER MATH assignment, perplexed. Margie sat across from her, reading a gossip magazine to Xavier and Christiahn. The kids sneaked, popping each other in the head.

"So that's when the Hager sisters decided to get hip implants."

"Does that mean they can run faster?" Xavier asked.

"No, baby, it just means they don't have to look like boys anymore."

"Ohhhh," they said in unison.

"I just don't get it," Kim said, frustrated.

"Get what, baby?"

"This. It's too hard." She showed her mom a long, complex formula.

"But you were always good in math."

"That was then. This is now."

"You just have to focus, baby."

"Mom, I know the difference between needing to focus and not having a clue."

"Well, I sure as hell can't help you. I haven't taken a math class in forty years."

"Was that during the Civil War?" Xavier asked, sincerely. Margie gave Xavier an unkind look.

"Yeah, boy. Now go clean your room, both of you," Margie shot back.

"What I do?" Christiahn said with a frown.

"Nothing. But I still want you to go."

Xavier and Christiahn got up and headed to their room.

"That's what you get for reading them those old history books instead of children's books," Kim said.

"I like history, and so will they when they get older."

"And gossip magazines, too?"

"Hey, you can't take life so serious."

"Whatever. Anyway, I haven't had a math class in seventeen years myself."

"Well, you better get a tutor."

"Yeah. I think the thrill of being back in school is officially over."

"Hey, I moved out of my house, so ain't no stopping now," Margie said with a bite. Kim shook her head, stressed, and continued to wrestle with the math formula from hell.

Chapter 24

THEO SAT IN AN AIRPLANE IN FIRST CLASS, ON THE way to one of his many book signings. He graded papers, trying his best to get them out of the way so that when he arrived in Houston he could just do the book signing and relax. Maybe even get a massage.

When he finished Kim's paper, he smiled, impressed. He marked an *A* at the top of her paper and moved on to the next one.

As he worked on the other students' papers, he could not help but think about Kim and what she wrote. She wrote about second chances, and how life experience was the greatest teacher if you're paying attention. Unlike the other students, there was wisdom in her words. And it made him think about his own work and journey. It also sparked an awesome idea for his new book.

That night Theo and Whitney talked on the phone, laughing hysterically. He told her how at his book signing, an old white lady asked him what was his favorite film he acted in. He told her how the crowd erupted in laughter, and how someone quickly told her that he was not Denzel Washington, but Theodore Washington. And that she tried to clean it up by saying *They all look alike*. He told her he just played it off by saying *Yeah, we do kind of favor*. He told her how the crowd laughed, knowing he was being a good sport about it.

The next day Whitney was at work, digging into a co-worker's ass. Her boss was watching from across the room, giving her the nod of approval. She continued to rip into the guy—yelling at him, telling him what she expected of him, poking him in the belly with her finger. The poor guy just stood there taking it, on the verge of tears.

Sam was witnessing it all while emptying the trash, trying his best not to laugh. He could not understand how someone would let another person abase them like that. After all, she was half his size and the guy was at least six-five, two hundred eighty pounds. Sam shook his head, amused, as he exited.

Kim lay in bed watching television with Lisa, Xavier, and Christiahn. She watched Theo… a guest on *Real Talk With Bill Maher*. Theo looked great, and very confident in what he was saying. He was also funny. He made everyone laugh, including Kim.

Theo walked off the set, happy with his performance on the show. A stagehand took the mic off his tie. Theo's smile slowly disappeared when he saw David on the phone, looking like someone died. He walked up to him, concerned.

"Okay, we'll be there," David said, now staring at Theo. He hung up. "We got a problem," he said, as he shook his head, bewildered.

Theo and David waited in the lobby of *Becks Publishing*, in a high-rise in New York City's publishing district. A beautiful woman looking like a runway model strolled out to the lobby. "Mr. Becks will see you now," she said, wearing a plastered smile.

"Thank you," Theo said. They got up and followed the young lady down the hall.

123

In the conference room eleven people dressed in suits sat at a long table, with the owner of the company, Larry Becks, at the helm. Theo and David came in, greeting everyone. They sat down, eager to find out what was so urgent that they had to drop everything and fly there right away.

"How you doing, Theo?" Larry asked, almost concerned.

"I'm fine, Larry. How are you doing?" Theo asked.

"Unfortunately, not too good," Larry said.

"Okay," Theo said, waiting for him to say what was obviously on his mind.

"All right, Theo, I think that I should just get to it. I don't want to beat around the bush. This marriage thing has kind of gotten out of control. Ms. Jordan Yikes. Your old girlfriend has caused quite a stir among your fans."

"Look, my fans see through her. She's just a bitter ex-girlfriend who's trying to get back at me," Theo said.

David leaned forward, wearing a sheepish grin.

"Just a bitter ex. That's all," David added.

"Well, bitter or not, she's creating quite a buzz," Larry said, letting out a big sigh. He turned on *Youtube*, on the flat screen on the wall. Theo and David looked at each other, perplexed and worried. "She's gotten nine million hits, from that talk show you did where she ambushed you. And now she's got another video with twelve million hits." Larry pressed play on the remote control.

They watched as Jordan vented. "I'll guarantee he won't get married because it's not in his personality. He's a phony. He won't allow himself to get married. Trust me, he will come up with some excuse not to get married, saying he changed his plan for some reason and how this is his new journey, and he's growing, or he'll say he has a family or personal emergency. So for all of you ladies that buy his books, thinking that he believes the stuff that he writes, mark my words. He will not get married!" she screamed into the camera.

Larry paused the video. Jordan looked enraged, freeze framed on the flat screen. People in the room snickered, giving each other comical looks. Theo looked at them, eyes narrowing.

"Goddamn. You really pissed her off," David said with a chuckle.

Theo looked at David wide-eyed, as if he wasn't helping.

"And you don't even wanna read the comments on her little ambush on *Wake Up America.* You gotta lot of pissed-off women out there, Theo," Larry said.

"Larry, you know this is going to blow over eventually," David said.

"That's what I thought. But it's not."

"Look, I can't be worried about that. My job is to write, not worry about being liked by crazy people."

"Well, you should. She's affecting your sales. And your fans think you're a fraud. So to make a long story short… You really have to get married."

Theo looked at Larry as if he could not believe the situation he was in. He felt like he was in someone's silly Hollywood movie.

"I'm working on it," he said dryly.

"Well, you better work harder. Or you won't have a deal with us come spring."

"Wait a minute, Larry; we have a contract that we're doing another book with you," David said.

Larry thought a moment.

"Sue me," he said matter-of-factly. Theo gave David a *what the fuck?* look. Larry added, almost amused, "Hey, I didn't know you would be on this crazy woman's hit list."

"Look, Larry, this isn't fair. I just bought a house because we had a contract."

"It's business, Theo," Larry replied.

"I got that. I'm just saying…"

"Look, Larry, he's going to be married, so there's no problem. Right now he's in love with this wonderful woman named Whitney. So what are we talking about?" David chimed in with a smile that said *no worries*. Theo sat there flabbergasted.

"Well, I guess we don't have a problem after all," Larry said, one eyebrow higher than the other.

Theo looked at Larry. Then he looked at David, who had a huge fake smile on his face.

"So does this mean we're going to get that advance for Theo's new book while we're here?"

"Fuck no," Larry said with a sardonic expression.

Theo looked at David as if his timing was terrible.

Chapter 25

THEO SAT IN HIS OFFICE AT UCLA, PERUSING PAPERS. There was a knock on the door.

"Come in," Theo said.

Kim entered, looking tired and stressed.

"Kim," Theo said, surprised.

"Hello, Mr. Washington. You busy?"

"No, no. Come in. And call me Theo for God sakes."

Kim smiled.

"Okay, Theo."

"So what's going on, Kim?"

"You were a math instructor for awhile, right?"

"Yes."

"Because I could use some help. I tried to talk to my math instructor, but he just makes it more difficult. And I signed up for a tutor, but I have a test tomorrow."

"Okay. Let me see what you got."

She went into her bag and pulled out her work.

He looked at one of the formulas. "Mmm. Mmm hmm."

"What do you think?"

"It's not that difficult. I'll show you some shortcuts that give you the same result, without all of the drama. Some of the professors, I'm afraid, are a little old school when it comes to these formulas."

"So you'll help me?"

"Absolutely. I have a meeting in the next ten minutes, but after that I'll be here."

"So, can I meet you in a couple of hours, 'cause I have a class that started five minutes ago?" she asked, appreciative.

"Sounds like a plan," Theo said, happy to help.

"Thank you so much. It's just…"

"I know, I know. I've been there. You get lost if you miss one move and it's hard to catch up."

"You're telling me."

"You must be pretty good at math. They placed you at a high level."

"Yeah, but to be honest, I'm on a time schedule. I can't be messing around taking lower-level math to catch up, and the counselor just went off of the last math class I took. But she didn't realize it was sixteen years ago…"

"I hear you. Come back after your last class and we'll get you all caught up."

"Two hours?"

"Perfect. I'll be here."

"Thank you so much."

"No problem."

"By the way, I saw you on Bill Maher."

"You did?"

"Yeah."

"How'd I do?"

"Good. But…"

"What?" he said, interested.

"Sometimes you talk over people a little."

Theo was taken aback. He paused before responding.

"My mother said the same thing."

"But, other than that, you were great."

"Well, thanks for your honesty."

"No problem." They both smiled as she rushed out to her class.

Chapter 26

KIM SAT IN CLASS TAKING NOTES. SHE STARED OUT the window into the night. Sighing, thinking. She looked at the young students taking notes. Some of them also drifting off. One male student slipped a pretty girl a note. She read it and blushed. Kim smiled and thought about what it used to be like, to be young with no bills and no worries, and boys constantly hitting on you. She remembered how it felt, to feel like she would be young forever.

She thought about her great aspirations, of one day being the CEO of a Fortune 500 company. She was driven and excited about life and what was to come. Even when she got pregnant, she found the upside to it and got excited about her new life as a mother. She figured she'd have her one child and then get back into school and continue on the path to greatness. She never imagined that her goals would shift from being a successful businesswoman to being a successful mother and wife.

As she scanned the class of young people, a sadness came over her. These kids had no idea how fast their lives would change. And how fast time flies. Some of them would let the pressure get to them and turn to drugs and alcohol. Others would have kids and have to settle for a career they once thought was beneath them. Some might realize their dreams, but at the cost of a wife, a husband, or children. And who knows. Maybe some of them just might get it all, the great career and the happy family.

She thought about how, at the age of thirty-six, she had managed to get back in college, working on a degree in economics while raising three kids. She loved her kids, but at times wanted to strangle them. She wondered if she was taking on too much and would fail miserably at everything—being a mother and going to school. She asked herself, *What the fuck am I doing here? I can't do this.*

She remembered when Thomas lost his job and they were evicted from their small apartment. And, just like that, they were homeless and living out of their van.

They couldn't go to Thomas's family because it was supernaturally dysfunctional. His grandmother who raised him had passed. And Kim's mom was too religious at the time. So they toughed it out for a few weeks, doing the best they could— sleeping in their van, hanging out at parks, and showering in local gyms. Thomas tried his best to find a job, but there was nothing out there. Eventually, Kim broke down and asked her mother could they stay with her. Her mother said to accept them into her home without them being married would be accepting their lifestyle and slapping God in the face. So her mother said no, crying the whole time. And, like that, they were back to living out of their van.

Eventually Thomas got a job and they were able to get another apartment. Two years later they got married.

It was late. Theo and Kim were working on Kim's math homework. "See, it's all about breaking it down a little bit at a time. Instead of thinking of this as one big problem, think of it as a bunch of little ones."

"Yeah," she said, her wheels turning.

"Do you get it?"

"I think so." She wrote some numbers down. "How's that?" Kim smiled as she finished the math problem. She pushed it over to him. He read it over and smiled, too.

"Excellent."

They both stared, impressed with each other.

"Thank you so much."

"Will you stop thanking me?"

"Okay, okay. It's just first with the ride, and now with this," Kim said.

"Don't worry about it."

They looked at each other for a nice moment. She broke eye contact, uncomfortable in his gaze, and quickly put her things in her backpack. They... felt the sudden tension.

Kim hopped up and all of her things fell out of her bag. Theo rushed over to help. They were on their knees and Theo looked up.

"Can I ask you a question?"

"Sure," Kim said, a little hesitant, as she continued to pick up her things. Theo thought for a moment before he spoke.

"Never mind," he said with a smile.

Suddenly things became even more awkward. Then, like a reflex, Theo kissed Kim on the lips. She was surprised, but kissed him back. Their lips, realizing what they were doing, abruptly parted. Theo looked ashamed and Kim a nervous wreck. She threw the rest of her things inside her bag and shot out of the office. Theo got up slowly and plopped down in his chair.

"What the hell is wrong with me?" he asked himself, letting out a huge sigh.

Chapter 27

THEO ATE DINNER WITHOUT A WORD. WHITNEY watched him, her plate already clean.

"Are you okay?" Whitney asked.

"Yeah, I'm fine."

She got up and started to message Theo's neck and shoulders.

"You got a lot of tension going on back here."

"It's not that bad."

"Yes it is. I can feel the knots. I know one way to relieve some of that stress," Whitney said with a smile, laying soft pecks on his neck.

"Oh, yeah? And what way is that?"

"You know." She used her tongue to lick the back of his neck, sending chills throughout his body.

"Oh, that. That'll do it."

"I know it will. That's what I just said. Pay attention."

She popped him on the side of his head. He gave a little laugh as she continued to kiss him on the neck. She then said in a sensual tone, now sitting on his lap, "I want you to take me back to my room and do that little ear thing I love." She kissed him slow and deep. When their lips parted, Theo looked uninterested.

Chapter 28

KIM SAT ON HER BED HOLDING A FRAMED PHOTO OF her and Thomas with the kids in the hospital. Thomas was bald from the chemotherapy. She focused on his smile, then on the pain in his eyes. She wanted to cry, but did her best to hold back her tears. She snapped out of her sadness when she heard a knock on her bedroom door. She quickly put the photo back on the nightstand. "Come in," Kim said.

Margie peeked her head inside.

"Hey, do you need anything before I go to bed?"

"No, I'm fine."

Margie noticed the family photo was barely on the nightstand and not propped up. She also noticed that Kim looked sad.

"Well, let me know if you need anything."

"All right, mom." Margie sympathized with Kim for a moment, then shut the door. Kim reached for the family photo, then lay back in bed clutching it to her chest. She finally began to cry.

Chapter 29

THEO LECTURED WHILE HIS STUDENTS HUNG ON HIS every word.

"So when you find that thing you love, and you pursue it with all your passion, and you feel like you were put on this earth only to do that... And it doesn't even feel like work because you love it so much. That's when you know you're in the profession you were meant to be in—if it's legal, of course."

The class laughed.

"And just don't forget about your spouse and kids. That's the easiest way for your mate to cheat on you, and for your kids to grow up on crack or meth."

The class continued to laugh.

"So, you definitely have to find a balance."

Theo gave a quick glance at Kim, who was enthralled. Her eyes quickly ran from his, pretending to write down some notes.

"'Cause life is short. That's why you have to plan, plan, plan… And for God sakes, separate yourself from the friends that aren't being supportive. People who tell you, you can't do it, for fear that you just might. Which would only make them feel that much more shitty about their own lives."

Students laughed.

"You have to move on. Because life and business are hard enough without the people around you bringing you down… And then you'll find yourself doing the worse thing a person can do to themselves. Compare themselves and their success to others. 'Cause someone will always have more than you. And if you buy into comparing your success with others you'll never be satisfied or happy. You'll be on fucking Face Book posting pictures of your life trying to convince others how happy you are. 'Look at me, I swear I'm happy! I swear I am… I promise you I'm so successful, just look at my friends and the food I've prepared for my family. I swear to God I'm so freakin' happy! Please believe me!'" The students laughed at Theo's overly dramatic plea. "Define your own success in life Goddamnit, and not follow the herd beating yourself up because your success doesn't look like someone else's… It's fucking exhausting and depressing… Trust me I know." The students looked on silent as if he had struck a nerve. Theo looked like he even had his on revelation. "So like I said, define your own success, that's the key to happiness… see you next week."

Students sporadically applauded and got up to leave. Theo saw Kim quickly gather her things and head for the door.

"Kim. Can I speak with you for a moment?"

Kim stopped by the door, a couple steps from freedom. She slowly turned, then headed toward him as students filtered out of the classroom. Theo sat on the edge of his desk. Kim took a seat in the front row. They both waited until the last student left.

"Kim, I just wanted to say how sorry I am."

"It's okay."

"No, no, it's not. I don't know what happened."

"Yeah, me either."

"Here I am, your professor, and you're my student."

"Well, it's not like I'm your typical student." Kim attempted to break the ice with a smile.

"But there's still no excuse. And also, I just wanted you to know that I have never, ever done that before to one of my students. I feel horrible."

"It's okay."

"You do believe me?"

"Of course."

"No hard feelings?" Theo asked, apologetic.

"None at all."

Theo smiled. They stared at each other for a brief moment.

"See you next week," he said, still wearing a smile.

"Bye." Kim started to head out.

Theo thought for a moment.

"You hungry? I have a gift card to a really great restaurant, and it expires tonight." Kim was thrown off. "You like seafood, don't you?" he asked as if he was asking a question about food, and not about her going out with him.

"Sure," Kim said, unsure what she was saying *sure* to.

Kids played wildly throughout the house while Margie helped Kim button up her dress. Kim looked stunning. Her hair was down and not in her usual ponytail. She was also wearing makeup, with lipstick that matched the red in her dress.

"Mom, I don't know what I'm doing. And I feel so bad. I didn't tell him my situation."

"And what situation is that?"

"That I got three kids and I'm in debt."

"What does that have to do with anything?" Margie asked, her face scrunched up.

"Nothing I guess, but…"

"Just go out and have a good time. That's all. Just have some fun. You deserve it."

"Do I?" Kim stared at her, looking for confirmation. Margie smiled.

"Absolutely."

"Well, hurry up. I told him to call me from around the corner so I can meet him outside."

"Meet him outside?"

"I just didn't want to… well, you know."

Margie looked around at their chaotic surroundings and nodded in agreement, amused. She took a look at Kim's shoes, liking the way they matched her dress. The doorbell rang. Kim froze and so did Margie.

"Oh shit," Margie slipped out. The doorbell rang again. Kim took a deep breath and inched over to the door, while Margie tried to wrangle the screaming kids out of the living room.

Kim cracked the door open. Theo stood before her in a nice sports coat. Kim squeezed onto the front porch and shut the door behind her. Even with the door closed, they could still hear the kids fighting and Margie trying to shut them up.

Theo was stunned by Kim's beauty. He snapped out of it.

"Sounds like a party in there. You got company?"

"No, not exactly."

"Oh…"

"I thought you were gonna call me." Kim said, wincing at the noise from inside.

"I did. You sure that battery isn't out again?"

Kim looked like it could be. They both stared at the door, hearing the kids inside getting even louder. Kim felt like she had to give an explanation for all of the ruckus going on inside. She hesitated, then thought *The hell with it*.

"Look, I have to be straight with you. You hear all that drama in there…? Well those are my kids." Theo's eyes showed his disappointment.

"Oh, you got kids. That's cool."

"Three of them." Theo's face dropped.

"You, you, you said three?"

"Yes."

Theo thought a moment, then laughed.

"You're just messing with me?"

"No, I'm not."

Theo realized she was serious.

"Oh… Well, that's cool." Theo's eyes contradicted his words.

"You know, we don't have to go out if you don't want to."

"Nah, nah. It's cool, cool."

"Look, you won't hurt my feelings…"

"I know, but it's cool. Let's go."

She saw in his eyes how thrown off he was.

"It's okay, Theo. This is a bad idea. I think I'm just going to stay home." Theo smiled inside, feeling like he had been let off the hook.

"You sure?" he asked. She smiled, seeing him give in too easily.

"Yeah, I'm… cool. Lord knows I got studying to do."

"Oh, how is that coming?"

"It's coming."

"Good."

They stood there at a loss for words. "Well, bye, Mr. Washington."

He gave her a look, noticing he was Mr. Washington again.

"See you in class," he said, with an awkward wave.

As he walked to his car, he took another look at Kim. All he could think about was hopping in his car and burning rubber out of there. Kim sighed and headed back inside. She closed the door and looked through the peephole. She smirked, seeing him quick step it to his car. She leaned back against the door.

Margie stood staring at Kim, bewildered.

"What happened?" Margie asked.

"Nothing. I'm just going to bed."

Before Kim could take her second step toward the bedroom, the doorbell rang. Kim stopped. She went back to the door and opened it. Theo stood there wearing an apologetic smile.

"Since we're already dressed up, makes no sense letting our gift card go to waste." He held up the gift card. Kim stared at him, perplexed. "I know you're hungry. You like lobster don't you?"

Kim thought about it.

"I can do lobster."

"Shall we, Ms. Jones?" She smiled at being called Ms. Jones. Theo smiled as well.

Theo and Kim enjoyed their dinner, surrounded by an assortment of stuffed seafish that lined the walls. Their faces melted with each bite.

"So then my husband passed and my finances quickly ran out. My mom moved in so I could go back to school. And now here I am, right where I left off sixteen years ago."

"Wow, that's a big ass curveball. But, hey, I have to say, I'm very impressed that you would go back to school after all that."

"Yeah. I mean how crazy does it sound for a woman with three kids and two jobs to go back to college?"

"It doesn't sound crazy. It sounds smart."

"That's just because you're not a mom. It's different for men."

"How so?"

"Well, when most men want to do something, they just do it. They don't have to worry about the repercussions of their actions."

"That's not true."

"Men all over the country are waking up and telling their wives and kids that daddy's got to go do something that doesn't benefit anyone but daddy."

"Okay, you might have a point." Theo smiled and sipped his drink. Kim smiled back. "So. How is that math class coming?" Theo asked.

"Are you trying to change the subject?"

"Actually, I am."

They laughed. "Honesty." Kim raised her glass to honesty.

"Well, I'm not going to try to debate motherhood or fatherhood with a woman who has three kids. Just a little over my pay grade."

They laughed again.

"Smart and handsome."

They both gave a little laugh. "So… You think I'm handsome?"

"Sure, why not."

"Nice."

They got quiet, then laughed.

"Nice? So you're more impressed about being handsome than smart?"

"Yeah. I already know I'm smart."

They both laughed.

"Well, to answer your question about my math class, yes it's going a lot better, thanks to you."

"Glad I could help," Theo said.

"Me, too, 'cause I was drowning."

"You weren't drowning."

"Yes I was."

"Well, for the last and final time, you're welcome."

They both laughed.

"Did I tell you my mom thanks you? Oh, and my kids thank you. Well maybe not now, but later they will."

Theo laughed.

"Face it, Theo, you'll be thanked forever."

"Glad I could be of service. Now for the love of God, stop it!"

"Okay, okay." She laughed.

"So what are your kids' names?"

Kim lit up. "Lisa, Xavier, and Christiahn."

"Wow," Theo said, taking it all in. He smiled, seeing the love in her eyes when she talked about her children. They stared at each other for a beat, then sipped their drinks.

Chapter 30

THEO DROVE SAM HOME, DROPPING HIM OFF BEFORE he went to Whitney's.

"God damn, three kids! And you kissed her!" Sam said, laughing.

"It just happened."

"Steppin' in shit just happens. And besides, I thought you were supposed to hook me up with her?"

"Yeah, well..." Sam laughed as he drank a cup of coffee. "I think for the first time in my life I was speechless," Theo said.

"Well, damn, who wouldn't be? Three kids?"

"Three," Theo said, bewildered.

"Were they all by the same baby daddy?" Sam asked tickled.

"Yes asshole. You know, you wrong."

"My bad."

"Her husband passed." Theo empathized.

"See, now I really do feel like an asshole."

"Welcome to the club," Theo said.

"Well, I guess Whitney's back on the top of your list now..."

"She never left it."

"Whatever. But I will say that Whitney is no joke."

"She still kicking ass and taking names?"

"With a vengeance."

They laughed. Theo looked in deep thought.

"I don't know. It's something about Kim, I just can't put my finger on it. She's got something."

"Yeah, three kids," Sam said with a chuckle.

Theo sat at Whitney's dining table, bored, as she vented. He was only there in body, staring at her mouth moving, hearing every other word. He tried to focus.

"Everyone knows that my cases were the hardest in the firm. It's bullshit," Whitney declared.

"Yeah."

"And he always gets the easiest cases, so obviously he's going to have one of the best records when it comes to wins."

"Yeah."

"Hell, we get bonuses contingent on our wins. You think I should talk to the partners?"

"Yeah."

"I think you're right. That's exactly what I'm going to do. Shoot, I'm trying to make partner by next year… You know what I'm going to do? Write a memo and send it out to all of the partners."

"Yeah." Theo stared at her with a blank expression.

The next day Theo sat in front of the class working on some papers. The students were taking a test. Theo looked at the clock on the wall. "All right, people, time's up. Drop your test in the box by the door and have a good weekend."

Theo and Kim made eye contact as they gathered their things to leave. She looked like she wanted him to ask her to stay after class, but he didn't. She walked over to the box and dropped her test inside. They gave each other a final look as she exited the classroom.

When Kim pulled up to her house she saw Theo's car sitting out front. "What the hell?" Her heart sped up and her palms became sweaty. She walked up to his car to see if he was sitting inside. He wasn't. She walked up the steps and went inside, perplexed.

Theo was playing with Xavier and Christiahn on the floor, showing them card tricks and talking to Margie.

"Mommy!" The kids rushed Kim with hugs and kisses.

"Hey, babies. What are you two doing still up?"

"Playing. Mr. Theo brought candy," Christiahn said with a goofy smile. Everyone laughed at her expression.

"Yeah, Grandma said we can stay up," Xavier added.

"Yeah, Grandma said we can stay up," Christiahn repeated with a silly smile.

Xavier rolled his eyes at the echo in the room.

"For a little while," Margie said.

"Staying up and eating candy. So that's why you guys are so happy and hyper," Kim said with a disapproving smirk.

"Hey?" Theo said with a smile.

"Hey?" Kim said returning a gracious smile of her own.

"I tried to call you, but you didn't pick up your phone."

"Battery keeps dying."

Kim and Theo looked at each other, at a loss for words.

"Well, we're going to go to the room. You went to the library afterwards?" Margie asked.

"Yeah. Where's Lisa?"

"Sleep," Margie answered as she gathered the kids together and headed to the bedroom.

"Thanks, mom."

"Bye, kids. And nice meeting you, Ms. Robinson," Theo said, giving a little wave.

"Nice meeting you, too, Theo. And call me Margie." Theo smiled at Kim, making note of Margie wanting to be called by her first name. Margie took the kids to their room. Kim stood there uncomfortable.

"You really do have some adorable kids."

"Thank you."

"How old is your oldest one again?"

"Sixteen. Did you meet her?"

"Yeah, before she went to bed. I didn't know sixteen-year-olds went to bed that early."

"She's got the boyfriend blues."

"Oh..." They both smiled. "Did it go by fast?"

"What?" she asked.

"Her growing up."

"You have no idea," Kim said, thinking about where the time went.

"Man, I bet your kids don't even realize how lucky they are to have each other."

"Were you an only child?"

"Yep."

"Me, too. It definitely is a different experience coming up by yourself."

"Hey, but at least we didn't have to fight over the bathroom."

"That is true."

They let the quiet fill the room. Kim smiled at the sound of Christiahn screaming at Xavier in their room. Then they both gave a little laugh as Margie shushed the two of them.

"Look, Kim. I have to say I'm a little confused about all of this, with you and I."

"You're not the only one."

"I don't usually hang out with my students. Actually, I don't ever."

"Like I told you before, I'm not the typical student." She smiled.

He stood there, examining her smile and charm.

"I have to say, I'm really digging you."

"I'm kind of digging you, too. But, hey, I got three kids…"

"Look. I was wondering, can we go out again?" Kim took a moment before answering.

"I don't think so. Hell, we're in two totally different places in our lives right now. And the last thing I want to do is complicate mine."

Theo thinks for a moment.

"Come on. It'll be fun."

"I think you're just trying to be the nice guy, that's all." Theo thought for a moment before he responded.

"Maybe I am and maybe I'm not. To tell you the truth, I don't know what the hell I'm doing."

"Me either. That's why I'd rather not."

They stood there, both at a loss for words. Theo saw Kim was just as confused as he was. He said to himself, "Maybe this is a bad idea." He scratched the back of his head. "Well, I just wanted to say hey," he said, unsure of anything.

"Hey," she replied with a wave.

"I think I should go. I do have a lot of work to do tonight."

They smiled and walked to the door.

"Kim, do you mind if I ask you something?"

"No."

"Do you know how beautiful you are?" Theo asked. She was touched. Margie gasped from the hallway. Kim cringed—embarrassed by her mom.

"My bad. Just going to bed," Margie said, out of sight. Margie slinked off down the hall to her bedroom and closed the door.

"You don't, do you?" Theo said, staring at her.

"I appreciate that," Kim said, charmed.

"Well it's true... Bye."

"Bye." Kim opened the door and Theo walked out. She closed the door and leaned up against it, letting out a deep sigh. She waited a moment then slowly opened the door to see him off. Theo was right there. He kissed her passionately and she grabbed the back of his head, pulling him inside. They made out, forgetting where they were. Suddenly they stopped, hearts racing.

They started to kiss again, this time slow. Tongues intertwined. His hands slowly slid down to the small of her back, and then over her ass. His hands seemed to sigh at the size and roundness of it. He squeezed it hard. Kim's knees got weak, feeling his strong hands cupping her butt, squeezing every inch of it. She stopped him from kissing her and stepped back in what looked like an attempt to cool things off. Theo looked apologetic, feeling like once again he crossed the line. She focused on his lips, as he licked them anxiously. She seemed to be unsure of her next move.

"Just be quiet, though, okay?"

Theo's eyes went wide, getting the picture. He zipped his lips shut and threw away the imaginary key. Kim took his hand and led him quietly to her bedroom.

They stood in front of each other in Kim's room. Slow music played in the background. They both took off their shirts and tossed them on the bed. They smiled. They both stood there looking at each other. Admiring. Kim started to shake, her nerves getting the best of her. Theo hugged her. They held each other tightly until Kim's nerves dissipated.

"I've only been with one man."

"That's one more man than me," Theo said, trying to ease her nerves. She gave a little laugh.

He kissed her on the forehead, then the lips as softly as possible. When their lips parted, he smiled and started on her neck, shoulders, then breast. He kissed her nipples ever so gently using the wet of his mouth. Her knees buckled this time, almost sending her to the floor. He held her tightly once again, guiding her on to her bed.

They made love passionately and slowly, eyes locked. They tried to be as quiet as possible being in a house full of people, letting out *ohhs* and *ahhs* that were beyond their control. Their expressions showed that whatever was going on between them was magical. A tear rolled down Kim's face. She quickly wiped it away.

"It's okay. Don't wipe those tears. They're beautiful," he said, as tears streamed down her face with an expression of elation.

They continued to make quiet love throughout the night, hoping no one heard them. Their passion for each other was something neither of them could have predicted. It was electric and wonderful in every way.

❧

Theo and Kim strolled on the beach, watching the sun come up. Kim wanted to get Theo out of the house before everyone woke up. She felt great, realizing how much she needed last night. Although she had no sleep, she felt alive and rejuvenated.

Theo on the other hand was even more confused. He realized that when it came to women, he knew very little. Emotions stirred in him he didn't know he had. He wondered if he was just being a little over-dramatic about last night. Maybe it was just good sex. He honestly didn't know.

They laughed and kissed. They realized they had an incredible amount in common. She loved the way he talked—he had a wonderful way with words. He spoke down to earth, but at the same time had an impressive vocabulary. She loved his passion, and the way he carried himself. She could not help but wonder if this was going anywhere.

That night Kim worked her second job cleaning motel rooms, singing with her earphones on. She played a lot of *Al Green*, letting each song dictate her emotions to the point of laughter or tears. She thought to herself she was losing it. *Theo is just a guy. Keep things in perspective.*

Theo showed Kim around his house, then ended up in his home office. She loved everything about it, but was especially impressed with how clean it was.

Theo jotted some things down on his calendar real quick. She looked at Theo's two books, sitting on his desk with a bunch of Post-its sticking out. She picked up *Five Steps To A Happy Fruitful Life* and looked around at all the plaques and pictures, admiring all of his accomplishments.

Theo's cell phone rang. It was Whitney. He didn't answer. Whitney hung up, sensing something was wrong.

Chapter 31

WHITNEY APPROACHED SAM, WHO WAS CARRYING some boxes while listening to his iPod. He took off his earpieces.

"Sam, can I talk to you for a second?" Whitney asked, looking like she had something serious on her mind.

"Yeah, sure. What's up?" Sam asked, giving Whitney his full attention.

"Well, it's kind of personal."

"Okay."

"Look. I know Theo is your cousin and all, but is something going on with him?"

Sam was caught a little off guard.

"Not that I know of."

"Sam... I know you would be the first person he would talk to if something was wrong."

"Sorry, but I don't know anything."

"Nothing?" Whitney looked deep into his eyes.

"Nothing." Sam's eyes went a little shifty, uncomfortable under her gaze.

"Sam. I'm a lawyer and a very good one. I can tell by your expression that you're lying. Now what's going on?"

"I need to get back to work."

"Look, the only reason you have work to get back to is because of me, so are you going to tell me or not?"

They stared at each other for a moment.

"Are we done?" Sam asked, one eyebrow higher than the other.

"I don't know. Are we?" she asked.

"I'm done." They continued to stare at each other, like prizefighters.

"If you did know something, would you tell me?"

Sam thought about it for a moment.

"No, I wouldn't."

"So, you do know something?" Whitney's eyes tightened, as if she were peering into his soul.

Sam smirked, amused.

"Hey, I'm not on trial here. And I'm not one of your co-workers that you can verbally beat up on."

"Are you sure about that?"

"Ms. Whitney, I got to get back to work." Sam smiled and headed off.

She stood there watching him, taken aback by his strength.

Theo was teaching his class, animated as usual and full of passion. Kim took notes.

"So, when you're waking up, in the middle of the night because ideas are coming to you constantly. And work doesn't seem like work. Then you got something. Even if you don't know what the hell you're doing. That's how the best ideas happen, when you're in discovery mode."

Everyone laughed.

"I'm serious. Most successful people didn't know exactly what they were doing, but had a burning passion for what they were doing as they did it." He thought a moment. "They found something they loved." He glanced at Kim then quickly looked away. "We live in a country that has gotten away from what success is. Let me just be clear as possible, 'cause this will be on your test. Success is not about making money, but about the lives you change. Hell, people on reality television shows get rich. Rolling in the dirt fighting, dehumanizing each other... Is that success? Is that passion? Or is that a desperation to be what people think is success at any cost? To achieve extravagant things? Or recognition? This country has become a nation of mean people, where to get over on your fellow man or woman is considered smart business. Don't get me wrong, having a lot of money is good. Matter of fact it's great. But it's not success. It's just… having a lot of money. Happiness doesn't come from your checkbook but from what drives you in life. Family, business, art, philanthropy… After all, when it comes to getting really, really rich, it's just luck. Lucky to have a special gift. Or lucky to have access to the right people. To be born into the right family. Or to have won the lottery for crying out loud."

The students laughed.

"People like to say, hey I worked hard for my riches. Hell, most people work hard and most of them don't make twenty million a year."

His students looked on, enthralled. Theo checked the clock on the wall.

"I tell you guys this 'cause some of you in this room just might be some of those lucky rich bastards one day. So pay attention so you don't be in front of your mansion, unhappy as hell, yelling, this cannot be it!" Theo exclaimed, overdramatic. The students laughed. Theo laughed as well. "We all have a divine purpose, and life is about so much more than job titles and money. So if you hit it big, call it luck or call it a blessing. I just think it has little to do with us, but the creator's ultimate plan. At least that's what I believe." Theo looked intense.

"All right, everyone, see you next week." The students all got up to leave. Kim took her time getting her things together, then strolled over to Theo's desk. A couple of girls looked at Kim, a little jealous. "Hey, you," Theo said with a smile.

"Hey."

Their smiles flirted.

"You like my sermon?" he asked, feeling he went off on a tangent.

"Praise the Lord!" They laughed.

"I found out that I have to go to New York this weekend, so I was thinking. If you needed any help in math, ask me now before I leave."

"Well, I'm sure I can find something you can help me with."

They laughed a little. Out of nowhere Whitney approached.

"Heyyyy," Theo said, caught off guard.

"Hey, baby," Whitney said, wearing a smile that screamed *fucker*.

She aimed that same smile at Kim, then gave Theo a kiss on the lips. She stood there staring at both of them, her fake smile waiting for one of them to say something. Kim was crushed, looking like a raccoon in that brief moment before it becomes road kill.

"All right, Kim. We'll work on that math later, okay," Theo said, a hint of nervousness in his voice.

Kim got the picture, staring back at him, baffled by it all.

"Okay, Mr. Washington."

Her sarcasm cut. He watched her walk away. Whitney stood there, hands on her hips, looking at him. In Theo's periphery he saw Kim take a final look back as she exited the doorway. He felt horrible.

"So what are you doing here?" he asked.

"I thought I would take you out for a late lunch."

"A late lunch?" Theo looked at his watch.

"Yeah, a late lunch. Or an early dinner. Or whatever you wanna call it."

Their eyes were saying so much more than they were.

"After you," he said.

They ate, feeling the tension.

"So, what's going on, Theo?"

"What do you mean?"

"With you. You've been really distant."

"No I haven't."

"Yes you have."

"Okay, if you say so."

"So is it because one of those little girls in your class? I saw the way they were all looking at you."

"No."

"Are you sure?"

"Yeah, they're just kids."

"Not all of them. Not the one you were talking to after class."

"Look, I'm not trying to have this discussion right now." She gave him the ni*gga please* look, then took her glass of wine and downed it. Her frustration grew. Out of nowhere she picked up a roll and fired it at him. He dodged it, falling back in his chair and knocking over a waitress walking by. The waitress dropped a plate square on his forehead. A few people screamed, startled. "What the hell is wrong with you!" Theo shouted from the floor.

"Are you fucking one of your students?"

A woman sitting nearby, covered her little boy's ears.

"What?" he said, a little dazed.

She picked up a water glass, ready to fire it. People gasped. Some even ducked.

"Will you put that away?"

"Who is she?" Whitney shouted.

"You need to go outside and cool off!"

"Mothafucka, I'm a lawyer. You can't bullshit a bullshiter. Now who is she?"

Theo moaned.

She put the water glass down.

"Kim," he said, almost under his breath.

Whitney was surprised that he gave her a name. Her anger grew. For a moment she was out of her own body, but she snapped out of her delirium, grabbed a ketchup bottle and cocked it, ready to throw. Everyone in the restaurant jumped and screamed. She caught herself.

"Will you stop that?" Theo shouted, holding up his hand to block her new weapon of choice. Whitney squeezed the ketchup bottle, holding it up, ready to launch it at Theo's head.

"Kim?" she said, as if the name left a bad taste in her mouth.

"Look, I want to be with you. She's just someone I was trying to help with her school work."

"Yeah, I bet."

Theo felt blood trickling down his forehead. He touched it and looked at the stain on his fingers.

"You're crazy, you know that?" Theo got off the floor and sat back in his chair.

"I'm not crazy, Theo. I just don't have time for no man's games. Like you, I'm on a schedule."

"Well what about you and your ex-boyfriend? The guy you had to be *sure* about. What kind of shit is that? And will you put the damn fork down?"

Whitney realized that she now had a fork in her hand. She calmly put it on the table next to the ketchup bottle. Her eyes were glazed over.

"I'm done," she said. She got up and stomped out of the restaurant. There was a sigh of relief from everyone when she exited. Theo sat there, undone and embarrassed.

Theo rode with David in his Porsche. He looked pathetic.

"How are you supposed to go on Piers Morgan with a big ole egg on your forehead? Put some ice on that thing as soon as you get home."

"Just get me to my car."

"I'm serious."

"Just reschedule."

"Do you really think it's that easy? Next week he's got Hugh Hefner talking about a new kind of blue pill he's been using called Apollo 13." He chuckled. "He says it's the rocketship that won't come down."

"Are you done?"

"What did you do to her anyway?"

"I told her about Kim."

David looked at Theo like he was stupid.

"Well, after she saw me talking to her after class. And after she tried to hit me with a roll. Or was that before?"

David laughed. He looked at the knot on Theo's forehead.

"That must have been a hard-ass roll."

"I knocked over a waitress and she dropped a… never mind."

"Wow. For a professor you sure are stupid. Don't you know you never talk to the other woman in public? And unless you're caught on the up stroke, you never confess."

"First thing. It's the down stroke."

"Not for me. I go up."

Theo looked at him as if he was not in the mood.

"You like Kim, huh?"

"We're just friends. Nothing's going to come of it."

"Only because she's got three kids." David laughed. "Holy shit, you trying to be like my cousin Hector?"

"No… I 'm not. How many kids does he have anyway?"

"A lot." David laughed. "So, what are you going to do?"

"I don't know… I shouldn't have been messing around in the first place."

"Hey, you're not married. Nothing's wrong with testing the waters."

"What the hell am I doing?" Theo said to himself.

"Well right now, you're bleeding from the forehead, which you wouldn't be if you'd denied everything in the first place. I don't care how many times she hits your ass in the head with a roll. You deny that shit. Deny deny deny." David chuckled, then stopped. He saw Theo was getting more agitated. "Hey, just be with the one that makes you the happiest."

"That's easier said than done."

"No it's not. You just have to stop thinking so much."

"Maybe that's why you've been divorced three times."

"You're a cold bastard, Theo, you know that?" David said, as if his feelings were hurt. Then he cracked a smile and they both laughed.

"I'm sorry… But seriously, I got the perfect woman in Whitney. With the exception of a few things. Hell, she was right to dump my ass."

"At least it was for something that you did. My second wife left me for cheating, and I didn't even cheat that time."

Theo looked at David, who seemed unfazed by his own words.

"I'm just glad I didn't get that woman pregnant. And she was trying, too. Did I tell you the time I caught her after sex, on her back with her knees in her chest in the fetal position, rocking back and forth trying to get pregnant? Man, I tried to straighten that woman out for damn near an hour."

"Straighten her out like how?"

"Her body. Stop my little soldiers from hitting that egg. You haven't heard that little trick that women do? I know it sounds ridiculous, but I'm glad I did it, 'cause she didn't get pregnant."

"You're right. That does sound ridiculous," Theo said, shaking his head.

Kim sat in her bedroom reading while Xavier and Christiahn played. Margie came in after the kids. "Come on, you guys, let your mom study."

"It's okay, mom," Kim said, letting her children jump on her bed.

"How's it going?" Margie asked.

"Pretty good."

"Are you ready for your finals?"

"I think so." Margie could tell that something was wrong.

"You guys go to your room so your mom and I can talk."

"All right," Xavier said, as he and Christiahn left.

"Is everything okay?" Margie asked, putting her hand on top of Kim's.

"Yeah."

"With Theo?"

"Sure. There's nothing there. We're just friends."

Margie could see in Kim's eyes the feelings she had for him.

"Well, you just remember. At the end of the day, he's just a man looking for a good woman."

"I hear you, mom. But I got…"

"Kids."

"Yes. Three of them."

"And?"

"And three kids are too many for any man. Hell, one is too many for most."

"Hey, if he's man enough for the job, it won't matter." Kim smiled, realizing how out of touch she was.

"I have to study, mom."

"I know. If you recall, that's why I got the kids out of here."

"I love you, mom."

"I love you, too, baby." Margie headed out.

"Mom, did time go by fast?"

Margie stopped.

"Why you ask?"

"I don't know. Never mind," Kim blew off her own question.

Margie smiled.

"Baby, it depends how you're living it. If you're living it badly, it could be slow. But fast or slow, it doesn't matter as long as there's *love and happiness*," she sung. As she headed out of the room, Kim pondered her mother's words. Thinking she might not be the only one listening to too much *Al Green*.

Kim strolled out of her math class, looking like she had a headache from numbers. She stopped in her tracks when she saw Theo leaning up against the wall. He approached her uneasily. "Hey, Kim. Can we talk?"

"Theo, you don't have to explain anything to me..."

"Please?" Theo insisted.

"It's okay. It should have never happened."

"Come here." Theo grabbed her hand and led her outside, toward a hillside on campus.

Theo and Kim stopped behind some bungalows in the Mildred Mathias garden. No one was around.

Kim folded her arms not mad at all, waiting to hear the explanation that Theo felt so compelled to give.

"Kim, I just wanted to say... I am so sorry about what happened. I had no idea she was going to show up like that."

"What's her name?"

Theo looked down before answering.

"Whitney. Whitney Mansfield."

"She's very pretty," she said with sincerity.

"Yes she is. And so are you."

"Well, thank you." She showed no emotion in response to his compliment.

"What is she, a businesswoman?"

"Why you say that?"

"I don't know, just the way she was dressed. She seemed very professional."

"She's a lawyer."

Kim listened, not surprised.

"I just don't want you to think I was playing you, Kim, that's all. And what happened, I'm just sorry about it."

"Look, it's fine. We never discussed whether you had a girlfriend. She was only your girlfriend, right?"

"Yes. I mean, we're seeing each other. But bottom line, I should have told you about her. I just kinda got caught up."

"Okay," she said matter-of-factly.

Theo tried to read her, a little baffled by her nonchalant expression.

"I just wanted you to know. I care about you."

"And that other woman?" Kim asked, a little curious.

"I care about her also."

Kim thought about his words, taking it all in.

"Look, Theo, I'm thirty-six years old. I'm a grown woman with three kids. No one's married here, and it's cool. You don't owe me anything. No one owns… anybody."

Theo stared at her, a little taken aback by her candor and her way of thinking. He timidly stepped toward Kim and grabbed her hand. She looked at her hand in his.

"What do you want from me?" Kim asked, staring into his eyes, showing a tinge of vulnerability. Theo thought carefully.

"I don't know…. Maybe to just be your friend."

"Then we're friends," Kim said earnestly. They stared at each other, not sure what to say next.

Theo and Kim made passionate love in Theo's king size bed. Theo studied the long line of Kim's neck as she arched her back with each stroke. They moaned in unison. Theo turned her on her back, putting her legs up on his shoulders. He looked down at her face, so beautiful and sexy he thought. He continued to make love to her, slow and forceful, giving her every inch of himself. Her head went back with each thrust. His hands grabbed her ankles, parting her legs then folding them like a beautiful pretzel. He sped up his movements, thrusting faster and faster. Words came out of Kim's mouth without her permission.

"Oh oh oh my my... God!" Kim screamed.

Theo stared at her, totally turned on as she continued to cry out.

This was a different person than the quiet woman he made love to in her house full of kids, he thought. She turned him over and straddled him, staring into his eyes. She placed him inside her and rode up and down, back and forth. This time Theo's head went back, jaws tightening with each stroke. He moaned. He tensed up. He shook. "Damn, Kim... you, are, killing me." He loved it.

"You sure about that?" She giggled.

"Yes... but in a good way."

They laughed, still in the throes of lovemaking.

"Oh… yeah," she said as she threw her head back, biting and licking her lips. Her senses becoming more and more responsive to his touch. Suddenly, her lower body jolted with pleasure. So did his.

They each let out a huge sigh of relief.

"Did you come?" Kim asked, still giddy from the incredible sex they were having.

"Not yet," Theo said, starry-eyed.

"Good." She maneuvered, reversing the situation, straddling Theo facing away from him.

"Oh, my, goodness," Theo said as she leaned forward. All he saw was ass. She rode him like the ocean, back and forth. Theo instinctively smacked her ass hard, making her ride him faster and faster until he couldn't take it anymore and climaxed. He let out a loud guttural sound. They laughed.

"Damn, you know you slapped my ass kind of hard?" She rubbed her sore butt cheek.

"I'm sorry. I couldn't help it."

They continued to laugh.

They lay in bed exhausted from their marathon sex session. They held each other, giddy and elated.

"That was great," Kim said.

"It was," Theo seconded.

"Yes it was," Kim said, acting like she was smoking a cigarette.

"I liked that little reverse move you did. I wasn't expecting that."

"I figured you'd like that, being that you always lookin' at my ass."

Theo laughed.

"You figured right."

They laughed, staring up at the ceiling, glistening from their workout.

As they lay in bed, each one wondered what was on the mind of the other.

"What are you thinking about?" Theo finally asked.

"How good this feels."

"It does feel good," he reiterated.

"I'm glad you came and got me at my class. I needed this so bad." Kim laughed.

They both let out a huge sigh, coming down from their sex high.

They continued to soak in the quiet of the room. Both of them felt out of body, loving the way they were feeling.

"I'm glad you came with me. You're amazing, you know that?"

"Well, thanks," Kim said, not sure whether he was talking about the sex or her as a person. She hoped he meant her.

Theo thought carefully about his next words and what he knew had to be said.

"Kim. I just want you to know… I just don't want to mislead you…"

"Theo stop. Don't mess this up. I have no expectations with us. I just want to enjoy the moment, okay?"

Theo didn't respond right away, taking it all in.

"Okay." He sighed and thought about the other woman in his life, Whitney, and what was to come. He glanced at Kim, who looked at peace and totally relaxed.

Chapter 32

LISA SAT IN BED, HORRIFIED, STARING AT HER computer. Tears flowed as she watched the worst thing imaginable—her and Kevin's private sex birthday video, sent in an email by Kevin. She had no idea how the footage could even exist since she watched him erase it before they left the hotel. Or did she? She saw him holding the phone, pushing buttons, but she didn't see the delete sign on the screen. She just trusted that he was doing it.

She hopped up and paced the floor, trying to figure out her next move. She felt like this was a bad dream, but it wasn't. Her face became flushed with humiliation, and her eyes filled with tears. She quickly got control over her emotions though. She rubbed her eyes, threw on a jacket and left the room.

Kim and Margie looked at each other as Lisa stomped through the living room and out of the house.

"Puppy love," Margie said. Kim gave a little laugh, with concerned eyes.

Lisa rode the bus, steaming, eyes red and glazed over. She looked like she was in a trance as she traveled from South Central LA to Inglewood. She got off of the bus and walked to Kevin's house, steaming mad. Her eyes went wide at the sight of Kevin's car in the driveway. She couldn't see him fast enough. Questions bombarded her mind. Who he had shown the sex tape to? What he planned to do with it? And what was the threat behind it? Even though they were not together anymore, she wondered why he would put himself out there like that. After all, he was on the video, too. Then she thought, he's a guy with no morals, he could care less. She started to have a physical reaction to the thought of all of this, and before she could get to his front door she puked.

She knocked on his front door, trying her best not to sound like the police, but her anxiousness came through. The door quickly swung open. It was Kevin's father. He looked at her like *What the hell is your problem?*

"Hello, Mr. Miles. Can I speak to Kevin?" she asked, a quiver in her voice.

Mr. Miles's face loosened up at the sight of her. His breath reeked of beer.

"He's not here."

She glanced at Kevin's car.

"Oh."

She looked confused, not sure if he was lying. She knew that Kevin's father was not the most standup guy in the world. She heard stories of how he had been to jail for domestic violence and had a drug problem back in the day. And even these days he could be a bit of a terror when he wasn't in a good mood.

Kevin talked about his father all the time, and how he wanted to be nothing like him. He had more respect for his uncle who sold weed for a living than he had for his own father. His father was indolent and trifling, and never held a job for more than a couple of weeks.

Lisa searched his eyes for the truth.

"You want to come in?" Kevin's dad asked.

The alcohol smacked her in the face once again.

"No, I'm fine. Just tell him that I came by."

"Okay." He smirked, as if it was no sweat off his back.

Lisa turned around to leave and he closed the door. She walked out front and sat on the curb.

Three hours went by and still no Kevin. She wondered if Kevin had got his father to lie for him, and he was inside the house.

It was getting late and her frustration started to fester. The fact that she was outside sitting on a curb, waiting to have an argument with Kevin, made her feel stupid.

She got up and strolled back to the front door. Just as she was about to knock, Kevin pulled up with some of his friends in an SUV. He got out looking like he had a drink or two. His friends were silly, loud, and basically assholes, too. They all saw Lisa and started to laugh. One of the boys said, "Ah shit, I wanna see this." All of the boys—with the exception of Kevin—laughed. Kevin smiled but had a tinge of remorse in his eyes, knowing why she was there.

"Let's take a walk," Kevin said, like nothing was wrong.

"Fuck you!" Lisa pushed him hard. The boys in the truck erupted in laughter. "What did you do?" she shouted.

"Will you calm down?"

"What do you mean, calm down! You fucked up my life! Why would you do that?"

"Will you let me explain?"

"Explain, Kevin? Explain how you ruined my life. And your own. Who have you shown it to?"

"Yeah, Kevin," one of the boys in the truck said in the tone of a girl.

Kevin looked at the guys in the truck, trying to save face, wearing a smile.

"What the fuck are you looking at them for? Do you realize what you did?"

"I didn't show anybody."

His friends exploded in laughter.

"Did that nigga just say he didn't show anybody?" one of the guys said. They laughed hysterically.

Kim dropped her head, ashamed. "Who are you?" she asked, stupefied.

"I just showed them the part with you in the negligee, that's all."

"What's wrong with you?"

"Will you just come with me?" He grabbed her arm but she snatched it away.

"I'm not going anywhere with you. You're a creep and an asshole."

"Then, why'd you come over?"

"I would have never thought in a million years that you would be this fucked up. I want you to erase it. Right now in front of me."

"No it's mine."

"Did you put it on the Internet?"

"No. Not yet. But I will if you keep trippin'!"

"Give it to me!" She could see the outline of his phone in his pocket, thanks to his skinny jeans. So she went for it. He pushed her back.

"Will you stop? Besides, you broke up with me for nothing."

"That was because you were cheating on me."

"No, I wasn't," he said with a straight face and lying eyes.

"I saw you and Tina."

"Saw us where?" he replied, with a *holy shit* expression.

"At the mall, Kevin."

Kevin's eyes showed his guilt even more.

"Well how come you didn't say anything? Or say anything to her?"

"Because I didn't want to embarrass myself, fighting over some dumb ass guy."

"Like I said, you could have at least told me why you broke up with me. You just cut off all communication."

"You damn right! I don't owe you anything."

"You could at least gave me the respect to tell me something."

"Gave you the respect...? You cheated!"

"I had to get your attention somehow."

"Kevin, erase it now!"

She went for his pocket once again and they started wrestling on the grass. She was stronger than he expected, but eventually he overpowered her and finally pushed her away. Lisa tried to catch her breath.

"I said no. Now will you stop acting stupid?"

Tears streamed down her face. The guys in the truck laughed while passing around a joint.

"This is the fucking best," one of the guys said coughing from the joint he just inhaled.

"I hope you get what you deserve," Lisa said, pointing her finger at him.

"Kevin, that's fucked up. Erase it," one of the guys in the truck said. They all laughed. Kevin smiled, trying to be cool as if he had things under control.

"Are we done?" Kevin said to Lisa, arms folded. Lisa's eyes narrowed.

"Yeah. We're done," she said.

"Bye," he said matter-of-factly, then looked back at his boys with a smug grin.

"My mom was right about you," Lisa said as she walked away.

"Right about what?"

Lisa shook her head and continued down the street.

"Right about what?" Kevin shouted again.

"Being a prick," she shot back.

Kevin's boys laughed hysterically.

Lisa was emotionally exhausted. She was so enraged when she left her house, she didn't take enough money for the bus ride home.

She thought about calling her mother to pick her up as it got dark, but she didn't want to have to explain what was going on. Her mother was the last person she wanted to find out about this. She knew her mother would be horrified by the video and want blood. And most of all she'd be extremely disappointed in her. After all, her mother had enough going on in her life. So Lisa continued to foot it. However, the more she walked, the farther she realized she was from home.

She thought about how her life would never be the same. She would always have that video looming over her as she went through life. Whether she went on to be the president of a company or President of the United States. It would always be out there to haunt her. And the more she walked, the more she thought about how stupid she had been letting him record her. She even thought about the fact that her kids might see it one day. She cried on and off as she trekked down the streets.

As she walked—lost in her thoughts—a man in a pickup truck pulled alongside her. She acted like she didn't see him, but didn't act scared either. She knew the danger of showing fear when you're vulnerable, and the best thing she could do was act like she knew everyone in the neighborhood so there was nothing to fear.

"You need a ride?" the shadowy figure asked.

"No, I'm fine," Lisa said, as if this was not the first time she had been offered a ride by a stranger.

"Come on. Get in. You shouldn't be out here walking alone."

"No, I'm fine," she exclaimed. She then waved at someone across the street, who had no idea who she was.

"Look, it's not a problem," the man reiterated.

"Thank you but no thank you."

"How far you got to go?" he asked.

"I'm almost home." She knew she was far from being home. "Hey, Ms. James!" she shouted and waved across the street to a woman getting her groceries out of her car. The woman looked at her, bewildered, but waved back anyway. The strange man continued to ride next to her, not saying a word.

"I said I'm fine!" Letting him know she was not a scared little girl, even though she was. He finally pulled away, she sighed with relief and picked up her pace.

Kim sat on the couch reading one of her textbooks. She kept checking the clock on the wall. It read 11:49 p.m. She was worried, wondering where Lisa was. Margie walked into the living room.

"Still no Lisa?"

"No. I'm going to give her till twelve, then I'm going to look for her."

"Okay." Margie turned around but then stopped. "She's probably out with her little boyfriend. You did that a couple of times when you were her age."

Kim looked at her mother as she went to her room.

Kim got in her car and backed out of the driveway. She drove down the street and made a left. Then a right. After a couple miles, she saw Lisa, walking down the street looking miserable. Kim swung her car around and pulled up next to her.

"Are you okay?"

"Yeah."

"What the hell is wrong with you? Get your ass in the car. You know you're on punishment?"

"Yeah," Lisa said, no fight left in her.

"Where were you?"

"Mom, please."

"What are you doing walking around at night by yourself?"

Lisa didn't answer right away, overwhelmed with emotions. Suddenly she busted out in tears. Kim stared at her, wondering what was wrong with her baby.

Chapter 33

THEO KNOCKED ON COCO'S APARTMENT DOOR LATE in the night. Coco looked like she just woke up, wearing a scarf on her head with no makeup, and silk Mickey Mouse pajamas.

"Hey, Coco. I'm glad you answered your phone," Theo said, glad to see her—or anyone for that matter.

"What happened to your head?"

"Long story."

"Come in."

Theo kissed her on the cheek and strolled in.

"You been drinking," Coco said.

"A little."

"A little too much?" she asked with a smile.

"Maybe." He shrugged, then smiled at her pajamas. Regardless of Coco's profession she was still a child at heart.

"Well, what's up, boo?"

"Nothing. Just wanted to talk to somebody. Get a woman's point of view."

"You want some coffee?"

"Yeah, that'll be great."

Theo watched her as she made him some coffee. He looked around at her studio apartment. It was nicer than he expected, but with a touch of ghetto fabulous. He noticed one of his books on the end table. He smiled.

She strolled over and sat on the couch next to him. "What's up, baby?" she asked, giving him all of her attention.

"I don't know. I felt like after all that great advice I gave you, you owed me some in return." They laughed.

"Ah, come here," she said, making light of it, pulling him to her. They laughed a little as she lay his head in her lap, rubbing it gentle. He looked like he was going to purr like a cat at any time. "Tell me. What's going on?"

"I have a dilemma. It seems as though my finances are not quite where I predicted they would be."

"What's wrong?"

"My money is short."

"How short?"

"Really short."

"Well, I don't do refunds." They laughed. "What happened?"

"I had a lot of my money in the stock market, and other different investments, that just went… bad. And I thought that I was going to be able to weather the storm with my new book contract, but I can't count on that anymore… Hell, the house I bought was too expensive, I owe more on it, than what it's worth. Realistically, I can't afford it. And I have so much money going out a month, it's just making it worse."

She continued to rub his head while his eyes opened and closed with each soothing stroke.

"If you get booted out of your house, you can always stay here with me."

Theo looked around, thinking it was a sweet gesture. Even though their taste in furniture was so different.

"That's nice, but I'm not quite there yet."

"I'm serious." She made eye contact, letting him know she was indeed.

"Really?"

"Really."

"Okay. Good to know," he said with an appreciative smile. "I have a love dilemma, too."

She looked intrigued.

"Oh yeah?"

"Well, I kind of have two women I'm seeing, and I'm not sure which one's Mrs. Washington."

"I thought I was Mrs. Washington."

He looked at her hoping he didn't hurt her feelings.

"I'm just playing." She laughed.

"Mmm," he groaned.

"So what's the dilemma?"

"I met a woman who is, well, a lot like me. Maybe too much like me. She's organized, professional; she's a lawyer, beautiful, loves sports. And then there's another woman, who just happens to be my student."

"Ooooooh," she said, teasing him.

"Hey, calm down. She's thirty-six with three kids." Coco laughed at his sour facial expression when he said three kids.

"What, you don't like kids?"

"Why you say that?" Theo laughed a little.

"She's thirty-six with three kids," she said, mocking him with her own version of his sour expression.

"Well, I didn't mean to say it like that, but damn, she does have three kids." They laughed again.

"Hey, my grandmother had eight kids, and she was the greatest woman ever," Coco said.

"Eight?"

"Yeah, eight. I don't know how she did it. To this day, my motivation in life is to take care of her. She's just... an amazing woman."

"One day you will."

"That's a big part of why I do what I do. For her."

Theo looked up at her, seeing the love in her eyes.

"Does she know what you do?"

"Of course not. I tell her I'm an escort. I escort lonely men to parties. Like you."

Theo smiled as she chuckled. He admired Coco but felt a little sorry for her. So much potential he thought.

"Yeah, but just keep in mind, there other ways to make money."

"Are you judging me?"

"Of course not, sweetie. I wouldn't do that."

"Good, 'cause you never know. You're a good looking man. You might want to go into my business with your new finance problems."

They laughed a little.

"It would make a great turn when I write my autobiography," Theo said, amused by the thought of it. "You're a cool girl, Coco." He smiled.

"And you're an okay guy, Theo." She smiled back.

"Who knows. Maybe you're the one," he said with a little laugh.

"I'm not the one. You're too OCD for me."

They laughed.

She kissed him on the forehead. He smiled at her, suddenly realizing that Coco was not a typical girl but an extraordinary woman.

Chapter 34

THEO STOOD IN FRONT OF HIS CLASS, GETTING ready to lecture for the last time. He paced, not saying a word. Finally he spoke.

"Well, this is it. With the exception of the final exam next week. I just wanted to say a few words before I let you guys out of here… I expect great things out of all of you. You guys are destined for greatness. Why? Because you've put yourself where great things happen. Where people strive not only to improve the financial quality of their lives, but also to enhance their minds. Now look at each other for a moment."

The students looked at each other, all smiles. One guy frowned at the girl next to him and she mirrored his frown, caught off guard.

"You guys are some of the lucky ones. So many people don't have the means or knowledge to get to college. But you're here. Learning how to learn. Learning skills that you don't even know you're learning. You have a leg up in life and some of you don't even realize it. Back in the day you didn't need a college degree to get high-paying jobs. Nowadays, let's just say it helps a lot. So you guys have to stay the course. And if you need to go for an advanced degree, go for it. Trust me, those two or three years could be the difference between making fifty thousand a year and three hundred thousand a year. So think about that when you feel like you don't want to go to school anymore. Think about your parents who sacrificed their own education for yours. And maybe you going to college just might inspire your parents to go back to school if they need to. 'Cause it's just not about making more money; it's about learning about the world and the people who live in it. And trust me, the world is changing in leaps and bounds everyday. You don't want to get left behind. So set your goals and bust your butt to achieve them. And who knows? Some of you may achieve a phenomenon type of success. But even if you don't, you'll still be living the dream. Doing what you love… I just want to inspire you guys to do great things, that's all. To be bold in life, without fear of failure. I want you to learn what's important in life. I want you to learn about history, so you understand why it's important to vote. And why it's important to be there for your kids, if you have any. And why it's important to find a partner to build a life with." Theo couldn't help but notice Kim's absence as he stared at her empty seat. "So think about how you're going to make your life important. Who you're going to inspire, or sacrifice for... One thing I've learned is that things are not always easy. Sometimes you have to tap into a power that you didn't even know you had to accomplish your goals. Sometimes it's not even about the goal... but the journey itself. That's what I'm truly learning this semester. I know I talk like I'm old, like I have all of the answers, but the fact of the matter is, I'm still learning just like you guys. Hell, I'm only thirty-two. I, like most of you guys... just want to be relevant. Relevant to someone... So, whether you become a mailman, lawyer, firefighter, nurse, banker, businessperson, artist, just be relevant to somebody. Because none of us do it alone. We all get help from someone. And the job that you get? I don't care whether you're sweeping floors or running companies. Just do the hell out of it. 'Cause someone will notice... and then you will be what we all aspire to be... relevant... Hope you guys enjoyed my class. And I hope I was relevant... It's been my pleasure."

The students applauded and rose to their feet while Theo smiled. He looked again at Kim's empty seat, concerned.

As the days went on, Kim studied hard. She looked like she hadn't slept in days, staying up late into the night then taking her kids to school in the morning. Her mother did the best she could to keep the kids out of her way while she studied. When her finals came, she was ready. The last test she took was in Theo's class. When she finished she gave him a cordial smile, which he politely returned as she exited.

Whitney opened her front door. It was Theo. They stood there for a moment, then hugged. He told her that he made a mistake dating Kim, and that he had been so stressed dealing with his financial problems. She told him she managed to save over a half a million dollars over the years, and that his problems were her problems now. And they would be just fine.

The next day Kim played with her kids. She looked happy, but tired. She put her hand on her head, feeling a little faint from the kids' wild play. She decided to take a nap. She slept for fourteen hours straight. Dreaming about bills, her kids, and Theo. She wondered how she could keep up this hectic schedule. She felt like she was drowning. Although her mother was a lifeline, she still wasn't enough. She hoped she could make it through another year and a half.

CRITICAL

Sam and Theo jogged in the park. Sam struggled to keep up. He was out of shape, but gave it a real effort. "Come on, Sam, push it." Sam ran until he threw up.

That night Theo and Whitney double-dated with David and a beautiful woman.

David's date had huge fake breasts that jiggled when she laughed. David stared at them, mesmerized.

Theo looked like he wanted to be somewhere else.

CRITICAL

Kim came out of the doctor's office, wearing a puzzled expression. Then she broke down and cried.

Chapter 35

LISA WALKED DOWN THE STREET WITH SEVEN OF her friends. She was fired up, but there was a tinge of fear in her eyes. On the other side of the street was Tina, the girl Kevin was messing around with. She had about nine friends of her own. She was taller then Lisa, but not as thick. Their high school was only a block away, so a throng of teenagers filtered down the street. Kids were excited to see a fight. Most of them had their cell phones out recording, yelling *You Tube, baby*!

Lisa was a little scared. She knew she wasn't a fighter. The last squabble she had was in the second grade. However, she felt she had no choice. Tina had talked about her so bad, saying that she was a ho, and that Kevin left her because she gave him an STD. Lisa felt like her good name was ruined and she had no other choice but to rectify the situation by whupping this girl's ass. She also had so much stress in her own life, she thought this might be just the outlet she needed.

Tina stepped out from the crowd of girls, giving Lisa a menacing look.

"You know you're gonna get your ass beat?"

"I'd like to see you do it," Lisa shot back.

The crowd responded with *oohs*.

"I just want you to know, after I fuck you up, I'm going to do this every time I see you hanging around my man," Tina said, hands on hips.

"First thing. He's not a man, he's a boy. A stupid one at that. And second, I wasn't talking to him, he was talking to me."

"You really expect me to believe that?"

"I don't care what you believe."

"Bottom line, you're a ho and everyone knows it," Tina said, playing to the crowd.

"No, I think you got me confused with your mama," Lisa said, steadying her feet, knowing that a mama crack typically sets a fight off. The crowd *oohs* and *laughs*.

"Cute. But we'll see how funny you are when I'm dragging you by your face down the street."

The crowd erupted with laugher.

"I'd like to see you try."

Tina stepped up to Lisa and stared down at her.

"I'll do more than try, bitch," Tina said, eyes narrowing.

Tina quickly took off her earrings and handed them to one of her friends. The crowd was excited, ready for a fight.

Lisa balled up her fist ready to swing. She looked around at the kids pumping their fists in the air, eager for the first punch to be thrown. Several of the kids had their phones out, recording them as they squared up, fists ready for battle. To Lisa this seemed like an out-of-body experience.

Kids laughed. Some clapped. Some made bets, putting money in a hat. Then Lisa looked at Tina, who was cussing her out, ready to throw the first punch. At that moment Lisa realized something important.

"I'm not doing this." Lisa stepped back. Fists down.

"What?" Tina retorted.

The crowd shouted its disappointment.

"You heard me."

"What, you scared?" Tina taunted.

"Whatever. I'm too smart for this. Unlike you, I got a future. I don't want to be a congresswoman or CEO with a tape of me fighting your dumb ass on *You Tube* like some idiot. Find some other fool to fight with."

"Fuck this!" Tina stepped to Lisa, ready to throw a punch. However, Lisa quickly turned and walked away. All of the kids looked disappointed and turned off their phones.

Tina stood there dumbfounded, her fist still balled up, watching Lisa walk away. She then looked at all of the phones being put away, feeling a little self-conscious.

Chapter 36

THEO AND SAM SAT ON THE SOFA WATCHING THE game. Theo looked burned out. He had a legal pad in his lap. On the top it read *Pro's and Con's of getting married*. He had a line down the middle with a long list of things on both sides.

"I think I'm going to ask Whitney to marry me this weekend. Matter of fact, after I propose, we're going to stop in Vegas and get married before we come back. You don't mind not being there?"

"I won't cry one bit."

"I figured you wouldn't." Theo continued to work on his list.

"She doesn't want a big wedding?" Sam asked.

"Nah. She said she'd prefer a Vegas wedding. She just wants to get married, too."

"I know David will be happy, for the sake of the book contract."

"Yeah, I'll surprise him on the way back."

"Maybe you really are perfect for each other." Sam laughed a little.

"It's time," Theo said with a smirk, not quite sure what Sam meant by that. He tapped the pen on his notepad.

"You've known her for four months?" Sam asked with a sardonic smile.

"When you know, you know. Hell, I wrote a whole chapter on it. *When You Know, You Know*."

"Just because you wrote a chapter on it doesn't mean you know what the hell you're talking about."

Theo gave him a sarcastic look.

Sam chuckled. "What?"

"She's even dropping hints, talking about her clock is ticking."

"The ole shot clock. I remember those conversations."

"But I do love her?"

"Is that a question?"

"Look, I need to step up, right?" Theo asked.

"Sure, why not."

"I mean, I don't want to be one of those guys scared to commit."

"Yeah."

"I love her, so I need to marry the girl."

"Yeah," Sam said, watching the game.

Theo looked at him realizing he's not paying attention, or at least not like he'd like him to. Sam could see he was looking for guidance and he wasn't giving any.

"Sorry."

"So I need to do what I gotta do. Hell, otherwise Jordan's right about me. And I'm full of shit," Theo said, looking for more than a *yeah* from Sam.

"Yeah..." Sam caught himself. "I mean, absolutely." Theo looked unconvinced.

"Hell, I don't know why I'm talking to you. I teach this shit."

"That's true. But like I said, it doesn't mean you know what the hell you're talking about."

"You know you're not helping?"

"I know. I'm just giving you shit. And the same attention you give me when I've already made up my mind."

"Whatever. I'm going to tell her to fly to New York for my book signing, and propose down there. Get married in Vegas on the way back and that'll be that."

"Hey, if you're sure?"

"I'm sure."

"Good."

"She's beautiful, got a great career..." Theo said, making his case.

"And no kids," Sam said. Theo cut his eyes at Sam, knowing where he was going.

"Yeah… I'm gonna do it. I'm gonna call her right now and tell her to meet me out there this weekend."

"Or you can convince Jordan to let go of your balls so you can get married at your own pace," Sam said with a wry smile.

"I could care less what Jordan does."

Jordan's front door swung open to reveal Theo standing there with flowers. "A peace offering," Theo said with apologetic eyes.

"For what?" Jordan said, not impressed.

"For us."

"If this is a hit, there's cameras all around here."

"I come in peace."

"What do you want?" she asked, arms folded.

"I want you to stop bashing me every chance you get."

"I'm just telling the truth."

"You're doing it out of spite because I broke up with you."

"So what if I am? You hurt me, Theo. And you didn't give a shit about it."

"I broke up with you 'cause I didn't feel like there was any future with us."

"That's because you didn't give it a chance."

"Jordan, when you know, you know."

Jordan gave a malicious smile.

"Yeah, I read that bullshit chapter of yours."

"Look, can we just get past it?"

"I'm over it. Matter of fact, I talk about how I'm over it, and you, in my new book *Step Up, Men*." She flashed a sarcastic smile. "Which by the way is being published by my new publisher. You might of heard of it… since it's your soon to be ex-publisher, Becker Publishing."

He stood there, stunned. Her smug satisfaction shone like a beacon.

Theo drove his car talking to David on the phone. "What the fuck is going on? How could they do this!" David was in bed half asleep.

"Just calm down. I'll call Larry today."

"No, call now! And tell them it's either her or me!"

"Just calm down. I'll handle it. But we're not in the best position right now to be giving ultimatums."

"I don't care. Just call him, David!" Theo hung up the phone and gripped the steering wheel tightly. "I'm so screwed."

Theo, now calm, pulled in front of a house down the street from Kim's. He wanted to have a conversation about what happened between them, but he also wanted the option of being able to drive off. He sat there thinking of what to say. He wanted to show Kim the respect of telling her that he would be getting married soon. He thought about how he felt about Kim and if seeing her would only make him even more confused. Or maybe there was just something in him that wanted to save Kim from a life of hardship. Maybe he wanted Whitney to do the same for him. After all, he had his own financial woes. An expensive house, bad stocks, and no advance for his new book unless he got married.

With his birthday approaching in the next couple of months, he knew what had to be done. After all, he loved Whitney and knew she was the perfect woman for him in the long run.

His phone rang. It was David. "So here's the situation. They claim that this was their way of putting a gag order on her. That is, if you get married."

"What do they mean, a gag order?"

"It's actually pretty smart. They figure, if you get married like you say you're going to, then they can make her back off. And she's got a big following of her own anyway, so it's win win. But if you don't get married, they'll just let you go and let her talk about you like a dog. Like I said, it's win win for them. It's actually pretty brilliant… Theo, you there?"

"Yeah. I'm just taking it all in."

"Hey, but none of this matters, 'cause you're going to marry Whitney before your birthday. Right?"

"Right." Theo nodded as if he had been reminded what his goal was. "Talk to you later, David."

He started his car and drove down the street. As he turned the corner, Lisa stepped outside her house and saw him.

⁂

Theo was packing when he heard a knock on the front door. It was Lisa.

She stood there, hands on her hips, feeling uncomfortable about being there uninvited. He was taken aback, looking behind her for Kim.

"Hey, Theo."

"What's up, Lisa?" he said. "Is everything all right?"

"Everything's fine." Her eyes said that things were not fine.

"You want to come in?"

"No, that's okay. Are you busy?"

"Just packing. On my way to New York. What can I help you with?" Theo stepped onto the front porch.

"I saw you by our house."

He put his hands in his pockets and let out an unconscious breath.

"You did?" he asked.

"Yeah."

"I wanted to talk to your mom, but then I thought it would be better to just leave things the way they were."

"Can I ask you a question?"

"Sure."

"Why did you even take my mom out?"

"Lisa..." he said, as if he didn't want to go there.

"You made my mom smile for the first time in over two years. And then you just disappeared. Why?"

"It's complicated."

"Is it because she's got three kids?"

"No. Look, Lisa, your mother is a very special woman. And she deserves a man that is going to love her with all of his heart. I'm afraid that I'm just not that guy."

"How do you know?"

He thought about her words.

"I'm just not." His eyes mirrored the sadness in hers.

"Well, I just wanted to tell you, 'cause I know my mother never would. She loves you. I can tell… I just wanted to let you know that."

Theo rubbed his head feeling terrible.

"I'm sorry for coming over like this. Please don't tell my mom."

"It's okay. And I won't."

"Have a safe trip." Lisa gave Theo a friendly smile, then turned and walked away.

"How did you get here?" he asked.

"Bus."

"Lisa?"

She stopped and turned around.

"Yeah?"

Theo closed his front door and walked over to her.

"Come on. Let me take you home."

"No, that's okay."

"You really are like your mother. Come on."

In the car neither one of them said a word. The more they drove the more Lisa's eyes welled up.

"Are you okay?" Theo asked.

"I'm fine."

"No, you're not."

"I am..." Lisa busted out in tears.

Theo pulled over to the side of the road.

"What's wrong?"

Lisa tried her best to get herself together.

"Can you just drive?"

Theo shook his head *no*, with a smile. Lisa looked at him strangely, then cracked a smile of her own. "Really," she asked. "You're going to strong arm me to talk? Look who's acting like my mom now."

"I just said I'm not driving." His eyebrow went up, as if it was out of his control. "Is it about your mom and me?" he asked, hoping it wasn't.

"No."

"Thank God," Theo said, relieved. Lisa laughed. "Well, what is it?"

She took in a deep breath before replying.

"Being that you're cutting my family off and I don't have to worry about you telling my mom."

Theo winced.

Lisa put her face in her hands. "Everything is just so bad. My life is a mess."

"Your life is not a mess. It's just in transition."

"No, it's a mess. I have a girl who wants to fight me. My mom is crying every night cause of how hard things are for her. And I have a crazy ex-boyfriend who made a sex video of me on his phone and won't erase it."

Theo looked at her, stunned.

"Excuse me. Was that last part to see if I was paying attention?"

"No, it wasn't." Lisa looked emotionally whipped.

"Goddamn," Theo said, to himself. He tried to clean his stunned expression up. "It's not that bad. It's gonna work itself out."

Lisa rolled her eyes.

"That's easy for you to say. Your ass isn't naked on video for the world to see, whenever some asshole wants to show it."

"So it's not on the Internet?"

"Not yet. He wants us to get back together, so he sent it to me in an email as a threat."

"Wow. What an asshole."

"Who you tellin'?"

"Did you ask him to erase it?"

"He said no. He wants to get back at me for breaking up with him… So now I'll have that hanging over my head for the rest of my life, hoping he don't put it on the Internet at some point. I don't know what I was thinking, letting him record me. I said no, but then he talked me into it by saying he would erase it before we left."

"Well, why didn't you make him erase it?"

"I did. He acted like he erased it."

"Lisa… never trust anyone with your future like that. Especially a boyfriend."

"No shit. I kind of learned that lesson, Theo," she said with a tinge of sarcasm as she wiped her tears.

Theo sighed inward, empathizing with her predicament.

"Where does he live?" he asked, with a no-nonsense expression.

She looked at him, baffled.

"Why?"

"Just tell me where he lives..."

Theo pulled off. He drove fast. "Tell me everything you know about this kid."

"What are you going to do?"

"I have no idea."

"Theo, just take me home. I don't want you to get in the middle of this."

"Don't worry about it. I'm just going to ask him a few questions."

Lisa sat worried, not wanting to deal with this at all. She imagined this whole thing blowing up in her face and her mother upset that she got her professor involved in her mess. And the last thing she wanted her mother to know about was her doing a sex video.

As they pulled up in front of Kevin's house, Lisa's nerves got the best of her. Her hands shook, and she had to pee really bad. "Please, Theo, let's just go. What's done is done."

Ignoring Lisa's plea, Theo parked and got out of the car. He marched up to the front door, with Lisa lagging behind him. He knocked.

"Come on, Theo, let's just go," Lisa pleaded.

"Relax. I'm just going to talk."

Kevin opened the door. He looked a little startled when he saw Lisa standing behind Theo.

"Uhhh, can I help you?"

"Kevin?" Theo asked Lisa. She gave him a nod of confirmation.

"What's up?" Kevin said to Lisa. She stared at him blankly, hands still shaking.

Kevin's dad stepped behind Kevin, looking agitated as usual. "What's going on here?" he asked, posturing behind his son.

"Are you Kevin's dad?" Theo asked.

"I am."

"I'm Theo. So look. Kevin, your son, made a sex video with Lisa on his phone. And now he doesn't want to erase it, even though he promised he would."

Kevin's dad looked at his son amused, wearing a proud but sleazy smile. "Hey, I say we let the kids handle it." He shook his head, ready to head back into the house as if he had better things to do.

"No, I think we all need to handle this," Theo said in a stern tone.

"Who the fuck you think you are, telling me what we need to do?" Kevin's dad said.

Kevin shrugged at Lisa, with a smirk.

"You sure you wanna take it there?" Theo's eyes narrowed. Kevin's dad stepped toward Theo. Lisa's stomach started to turn, seeing a bad situation get worse.

"Man, I will fuck you up," Kevin's dad slurred.

"No, you will *try* to fuck me up. But here I am. Waiting for your next move."

Kevin's dad pauses for a moment, taken aback by Theo's calm demeanor and the strength in his eyes.

"Who are you again?"

"Theo."

"So what's this got to do with you? I know you're not her father."

Lisa's eyes tightened, her nerves turning into anger.

"I'm a close friend of the family. And I'm a lawyer, who has enough friends in high places to sue your ass for everything you got, and have you in litigation for the rest of your life."

Kevin's father looked beyond Theo, at his BMW.

Theo gave Lisa a knowing wink that he was bluffing about being a lawyer. "Kevin, you were intimate with this young lady and recorded it with the agreement that you would erase it right after. But you lied and did what you did."

Kevin's eyes got shifty, letting his nerves get the best of him.

"Then you sent it to her in an email, using your own email account, and threatened to send it out to the world because she broke up with you… That's low, Kevin. So here's the situation. You're going to go in your house and get your little phone and computer and bring it out here, and let us watch you erase every trace of that video. Or I'm going to call some of my attorney friends and we are going to file for an injunction, and sue you and your father for emotional distress."

"You can't sue me. I didn't do anything," Kevin's father said, unsure.

"Sure I can. Might not win, but I'll do it anyway, costing you thousands of dollars in lawyer fees."

Kevin's dad looked at his son in disgust. "Oh, and Kevin. We'll also be filing charges against you for statutory rape and child pornography."

"What?" Kevin said shocked.

"Yeah. Lisa's sixteen and you were eighteen when this happened. It was your birthday, remember? And thanks to your email, we have proof. And putting a minor on the Internet, is child pornography. Hope you like prison."

"I never sent it to anyone. Nobody has it but me!" Kevin exclaimed, scared.

"I hope not. For your sake. So why don't you go get your phone and computer and anything else you got that recording on. Or do you wanna try me?"

Kevin looked stunned, standing with his mouth open. He blinked out of his trance and looked at Lisa, who wore a smile.

"Boy, go get the shit!" Kevin's dad snapped.

Kevin rushed into the house while Lisa and Theo waited with their arms folded. Theo gave Lisa another wink. She was in awe of Theo.

⸙

Theo sat in first class, while the other passengers got ready for take-off. He saw a couple with two children ready to snap. The kids were five and three, and they were headed back to coach. He watched the stressed-out father trying to wrangle his kids to the back of the plane.

"And that's only two. Jeez," he said to himself. He leaned back and let out a huge sigh.

⸙

Kim was on her bed in the fetal position crying when Margie passed by her closed door. Kim had reached the nadir of her suffering. Margie stopped and leaned her ear toward the door, hearing a whimper.

"Kim?"

"Yeah, mom?" Kim quickly tried to compose herself. "Come in."

Margie slowly opened the door, peeking inside. "Are you okay?" Margie knew something was definitely wrong.

"Not now, mom."

"Baby, what's wrong?" she asked, in more of a stern tone this time.

"Can we just talk later?"

"No. You need to tell me what's going on. You're scaring me. Is it about Theo?"

"Mom, please."

"Kim, if you don't tell me why you're crying…"

"I'm pregnant, okay?"

"Shit!" Margie said. She felt embarrassed by her response. "Please, God, forgive me," she said, holding her right hand up.

"Yeah. Shit is right," Kim said, taken aback by her mother's language and reaction.

"How the heck you get pregnant?"

Kim shot her a look.

"Okay, got that part."

Kim sat on the bed, her face in her hands. Margie sat down next to her and put her face in her hands, too. Kim realized her mother was taking this harder than she was and rolled her eyes.

"What's wrong with me? It's like I'm cursed."

"Well, did you use a…"

"Yes. Hell yes!"

"Damn!" Margie blurted out. "Lord." Margie's right hand shot up.

"Mom, you're not helping."

"I'm sorry. Well, does he know?"

"No."

"What are you going to do?"

"I don't know."

"You got to tell him."

"I want to tell him so bad, but I just don't know how. Hell, I can see me in the paper already. *Successful author gets in over his head when he knocks up a woman who already has three kids*."

Margie put her arm around Kim, rubbing her back and doing her best to comfort her.

"Mom, stop rubbing my back. It's not helping."

"Well, hell, rub *my* back."

Kim gave a little laugh and rubbed her mother's back.

"Baby, look. Just call the man and tell him."

"I can't. At least not right now. I need to do this in my own time… My life is falling apart and I can't catch a break."

"Oh, baby. I'm so sorry," Margie said. She began to cry. Kim shook her head amused as her mother sobbed uncontrollably.

∙❧∙

Theo talked quietly on his cell phone in a bookstore, while people sat in chairs waiting for him to speak. "You just touched down. Great... I know, it's raining pretty hard... No, you don't need to try to make this. Just go to the hotel and chill out, then meet me at the restaurant... All right... Love you, too."

Theo hung up and headed to the podium. He held a copy of his book, *Five Steps To A Happy Fruitful Life*, with Post-its sticking out of the different chapters. The bookstore manager walked up to him. He looked very rough around the edges, with a lot of piercings in his ears and nose. However, he spoke in a high voice and was extremely gay.

"Are you ready, Mr. Washington?"

Theo was thrown off a bit. "Sure."

The bookstore manager stepped up to the podium and leaned into the microphone.

"All right everyone. Introducing Mr. Theodore Washington!" he said with glee.

Theo gave him a cordial smile, then stepped up to the podium and opened his book. An index card fell out and onto the floor. Theo picked it up. It had been kissed with lipstick, and it read, *You just might be my fifth step! Sincerely, Kim.*

Chapter 37

THEO SAT BY THE WINDOW IN AN UPSCALE HIGH-RISE restaurant. He stared out the window at the city lights of New York. Theo loved the view. He watched the rain falling hard, and the shafts of lightning. He held a ring box in his hand.

An overly giddy waitress approached, wearing a huge smile. "Everything okay, Mr. Washington?"

"Everything's fine," Theo replied.

"All right. You just let me know if you need anything. And don't worry, everything is set up to perfection. I just love proposals."

Theo gave her his traditional, cordial smile.

"Thank you." His eyes drifted back out to the view.

Theo sat there waiting. He put the ring box in his pocket. There was a nice moment of him just sitting there, observing his surroundings. He looked at a few happy couples eating. Then he noticed a few not so happy couples. He wondered which one would he be, ten years from now.

Whitney strolled in, dripping wet. She caught his eyes. The dampness of her skin made her look even more stunning than normal. Theo acknowledged how beautiful she was with a smile. She smiled back. He got up and gave her a hug and a kiss on the lips. He pulled out her chair and seated her.

"Hey, baby. Sorry I'm late. I took a nap," Whitney explained.

"It's okay. You look beautiful."

"Thank you. The food smells good in here."

"It's the best restaurant in the city, hands down."

"Well good, because I'm starving."

He smiled, knowing her love for food.

"How was your flight?" he asked, a little nervous, thinking about the ring in his pocket. It felt like it weighed a ton.

"It was good," she said.

"Great."

"I was working on this case the whole time, so the flight went fast. Plus Kramer was blowing me up with emails, mad because I took his name off the case. No bonus for him." She chuckled.

"Why is that?"

"Because I took his name off of the case and put my name on it. One of the perks of me being a senior attorney and him a junior one."

"That's kind of messed up," Theo said, uneasy.

"Hey, like your book says—seize the moment at all times."

"That's not what I meant."

"Yes it is. Remember, no one is going to give you anything. You have to take it," she quoted his book with sarcasm.

Theo thought about it.

"Theo, you forget. I'm a lawyer. I not only know how to read, but I know how to read between the lines."

He wiped the beads of sweat off his brow.

"Are you okay?" she asked.

"I'm fine."

Theo let out a huge sigh, almost as if he was keeping himself from passing out. The overly giddy waitress approached wearing a huge smile. She spoke like a flight attendant tending to children.

"Hello! You look so beautiful. Would you like something to drink?"

"Just water for now," Whitney answered, looking at her oddly.

"Are you sure you don't want any wine? Our red is to die for. Might I suggest our 2008 Cakebread Cabernet," the waitress said, overly dramatic, wearing a ridiculous smile.

Whitney looked at Theo like *Is this woman on crack or what?*

"Okay, no wine," the waitress said, then spoke as if she were talking to a baby. "But if you change your mind, you, just, let, me, know."

Whitney looked at her as if she were out of her mind.

The waitress gave a wink and sauntered off.

Whitney rolled her eyes and looked at Theo.

"What's her problem?"

"I don't know. But look, I need to ask you something now. Because my nerves are just getting worse." He thought for a bit. His eyes started to flutter as he swayed back and forth in his chair. His head was light and his mouth was getting dryer and dryer. "You know, I got to go to the restroom."

"Theo, if you're going to ask me to marry you, just ask."

"Excuse me?"

"Theo, I know that's why you asked me to fly out here. Nice restaurant, overlooking New York City. And your deadline approaching. It's kind of obvious."

He sat speechless.

"I'll be back." He got up and quickly headed off.

Whitney sat there bewildered.

Theo entered the restroom and started to pace. He then went to the sink, splashed some water in his face… drank a little out of his hands. He looked into the mirror as water dripped off of his face. "What am I doing? Damn." He whipped out his cell phone and called Sam.

"Hello," Sam said.

Theo smiled, with relief.

"Good, you're there."

"Yeah I know. What's up?"

"I'm about to ask Whitney to marry me."

"And?"

"And?"

"Well, what are you talking to me for?" Sam said matter-of-factly.

"I don't know."

"Isn't that the whole point of her coming up there?"

"Yeah, but I'm not sure anymore."

"Well you better be sure, 'cause you don't want to piss her off. Shit, she probably assumes you're going to propose anyway, being you told her to fly out there," Sam said with a hint of amusement.

Theo rolled his eyes, knowing Sam was right. He thought about the consequences if this didn't go smoothly and couldn't help but to laugh himself. Theo stood there confused.

"I just can't get Kim out of my head."

Sam took a moment before answering. Theo continued to stare at his reflection in the mirror, almost as if he was searching for something.

"Well bring your ass home and tell her."

"It's not that simple."

"Why? Because she's got three kids?"

"No, that's not it."

"C'mon, man, who you think you foolin'? I know your ass." Theo looked at himself in the mirror holding the phone. "Look, man, just follow your heart, because at the end of the day you're going to have to live with your choice. Literally. And life is too short to make mistakes you know you're making."

Theo looked into the phone, surprised by Sam's words of wisdom.

"That was good. You mind if I steal that for my new book?"

"Sure, it's yours."

"Thanks." Theo sat on the phone letting it sink in.

"Hey, sometimes people just need to hear what they already know."

"Well, thank you very much, Dr. Phil. I got all these Dr. Phils in my life… I gotta go."

"All right. I'll send you the bill," Sam said without missing a beat.

Theo smiled and hung up. He looked at his reflection as if he was trying to look deep within. He then straightened himself out and walked out of the restroom.

He headed back toward the table like a man with a cause bigger than himself.

Whitney saw him approaching and smiled. But then, reading his expression, her face turned concerned. "Is everything all right?" she asked.

He thought for a moment before answering. He sat down. Suddenly his phone rang. He glanced at the number. It was Kim. His heart nearly stopped. He looked at Whitney, who was staring at him like *What the fuck is going on?*

"Hold on, I have to take this." He got up and headed back to the restroom. "Hello?" He entered the restroom.

"Theo?" Kim said.

"Yeah, Kim," he replied.

"Hey?"

"Hey? What's up?"

"I just wanted to talk to you. And tell you I'm not meant to be with you and I know that. And I wish you the best in life. We're not meant to be together… I just thought you should know. "

"Why are you saying this?"

"'Cause I don't want you to ever feel like I was trying to trap you. I know we're wrong for each other. Hell, you and that woman look like you're perfect for each other. Besides, you're not even my type of guy… I mean, not like that, but you're not, and I wish you the best… but I had to tell you…"

"Look, I'm in the middle of something. I gotta call you back." He hung up, devastated and perplexed. He once again stared in that familiar mirror. He looked relieved. Like a hundred pound weight had been lifted off of his shoulders and things were back on track. Kim saying they were not meant to be together made his decision that much easier.

He strolled back to his seat, with Whitney staring at him. "Is everything okay?"

Theo stared at her a nice moment, knowing his decision was now clearer than ever.

She waited as he struggled with his approach. Finally, he just said it.

"You're perfect, Whitney. You're just not perfect for me."

"Excuse me?" she said, not believing what she just heard.

"I'm in love with another woman."

She stared at him dumbfounded, her anger brewing. Suddenly she grabbed the saltshaker, but he grabbed her hand, creating a loud thump on the table. Everyone in the restaurant stared, hearing the commotion. "Damn, you really like to throw stuff." Their waitress looked on like everyone else.

"Fuck you! You might be the stupidest man I've ever met!"

"Maybe so. But I can't help the way I feel... I'm sorry... I really am."

"Well, I'm just sorry I wasted my time! Matter of fact, I wouldn't be with your ass for a million dollars!"

Theo sat there, understanding she was hurt.

"And to think I felt sorry for your broke ass!"

"Really? You going there?"

"Broke, broke, broke!" she said with more and more disdain.

"Are you done?"

"And my stupid ass, telling you I got you. Don't worry about it? Well fuck you! I hope that girl Jordan ends your career. I see why she hates you."

Theo empathized with her, seeing her tear up.

"Whitney, I know you're hurt. I just don't want us to make a huge mistake..."

"Just get the hell out of my face. You lucky I don't get my brothers to come down here and fuck you up! Wasting my time, flying out here, for you to tell me this," she said, eyes narrowed and nostrils flared like a bull seeing its target.

"I'm sorry." He could see the anger and pain in her eyes.

She waved her hand at him, *in a get the fuck out of here*, kind of way. "I never meant to hurt you," he reiterated. He got up and walked out of the restaurant, leaving Whitney sitting there fuming. The waitress approached, disgusted with Whitney's behavior.

"You could have just said no," the waitress said.

"Bitch, get your kooky ass out of my face!" Whitney snapped, throwing the saltshaker at her. The waitress screamed and ran off horrified.

Whitney sat there piqued, then pulled out her phone and called her ex-boyfriend. She rolled her eyes at onlookers as she waited. When he answered, she smiled as if nothing had happened.

Theo walked the crowded streets of New York City in the rain. He looked tense, then a smile crept across his face. He started to run, looking like a man who had just been set free—from not only the wrong woman but also from himself. For the first time in his life he knew what it felt like to truly love a woman.

Chapter 38

KIM AND LISA SAT ON THE SOFA, COVERED WITH blankets, watching television. The doorbell rang. They both looked concerned and looked at the clock on the wall that read 12:37 a.m. "Who the hell is that?" Kim asked.

"Don't look at me."

"Better not be Kevin's ass."

"I'll get it," Lisa said, thinking it could be him.

"No. I got it." Kim went to the door. "Who is it?" Kim asked in a way that could be taken as *Who the fuck is at my door at this time of night?*

"Theo."

"Theo?" Kim opened the door.

He stood there, wearing an apologetic smile.

"I tried to call, but your phone. You really need to get that fixed."

"Oh. I know."

"I'm sorry it's so late, but I need to talk to you." He saw Lisa behind her. He gave her a wave. She waved back, hoping he wasn't there to talk about their little adventure.

"Come in," Kim said, baffled. He entered. Lisa went to her bedroom giving them some privacy. "What's going on?" Kim asked.

"I just wanted to see you."

She took a moment before responding.

"Why?"

Lisa watched from the hallway, trying not to be seen. Margie walked up behind Lisa, startling her, then taking a peek as well.

Theo stood there, hands in his pockets, searching for the words that would express how he felt. Suddenly a calmness came over his face. "So, I could tell you… I love you," he said, looking deep into her eyes.

"What?"

"I said, I love you. And I can't stop thinking about you."

"Look, you don't have to…"

"Yes I do. Because if I don't, I'll regret it the rest of my life… You're everything I've ever wanted. You're smart, funny, beautiful, and most of all, precious. And when I'm around you, I feel like I have a purpose. I feel like… I feel like, I have the perfect woman for me... I grow more when I'm around you."

Kim looked stunned.

"I don't know what to say."

"We both know that your little call was bullshit. We have something special. We both felt it the first time we made love. I may not have been able to explain it. But I've been with enough women to know there is something freakishly magical when it comes to us."

"I still don't know what to say."

Xavier and Christiahn were watching from the hallway too now, all trying not to be seen.

"Say you love me back."

Kim's eyes started to well up.

Theo stepped up closer to her.

She hesitated before she spoke, staring back into his eyes.

"I love you back," she said as if her heart was melting.

They laughed, amused by her response.

Tears fell from her eyes. She tried to wipe them but he stopped her. Kim gave a little smile.

"I have to get my eyes checked. I am crying entirely too much."

"You don't have to ever wipe your tears around me. They're beautiful."

Kim stood there, tears streaming down her face. She tried to wipe them out of habit, but he stopped her again.

"I feel silly."

"You're not silly." Theo kissed her on the lips. "Look, I know for a woman with kids, it's nothing to take lightly when falling in love. But I'm telling you, if you give me a chance, I'll prove that I'll love your three kids just as much as I love you."

"Five kids," Kim said, with a sorrowful smile.

The kids looked on, confused. Xavier and Christiahn counted with their fingers. Margie smiled, knowing about the new additions. Lisa covered her mouth in shock.

"But I thought you said you only had three?" Theo said, bewildered.

"Well, I got five," Kim answered. Theo's eyes fluttered.

"Okay, five. When do I meet the other two?"

"In about eight months." He still didn't get it. She looked at him lovingly, hoping for him to be okay with it. She rubbed her belly.

"What?" he said still confused.

She rubbed her belly again with a nervous smile.

"Oh my God…" Theo passed out and crashed into a glass coffee table.

He came to, lying on the floor amongst broken glass. Margie and the kids were all fanning him with magazines and sofa cushions.

"I'm going to be a daddy?" His mind still running on rewind. "And twins?"

"Yes. Is that okay?" Kim asked.

"That wasn't in my plan, but, but…" A huge smile slowly spread across his face. "That's more than okay. Come here."

"Some curveball, huh?" Kim said, feeling out of body about it as well.

"Absofuckinglutely." They all laughed. Kim carefully bent down and they kissed amongst the broken glass.

"Abso…" Christiahn shouted. Lisa covered her mouth, not letting her finish. They all laughed.

Theo and Kim continued to kiss, trying to contain their laughter.

When their lips parted, "Let's get married as soon as possible," escaped Theo's mouth. Kim and her family were in shock. Then a smile slowly came across her lips, cheeks, and eyes.

Chapter 39

THE NEXT DAY LISA WAS ON HER COMPUTER. SHE googled *Theodore Washington*. She saw all of the good comments that came up about him and his books. She saw the many television interviews and book signings on *YouTube*. She read his biography on Wikipedia. She was impressed. She wore a smile as she read about his achievements and awards. She felt a little guilty about doing a background check on Theo, but after all he was going to marry her mother. As she continued to read all about him on the Internet, she came across Jordan Yikes. Her smile disappeared.

She told her mother what she discovered, and watched her mother's smile disappear as well. Kim knew about the bitter Jordan Yikes, but not about the book contract Theo would lose if he didn't get married before his birthday. She felt played and betrayed. But most of all conflicted. She thought their love for each other was real. At least it was to her.

Kim and Lisa went to Theo's home to see him. Kim wanted to go by herself but Lisa insisted she go for moral support. He wasn't there. Lisa pulled out Theo's manager's office phone number and address. Kim looked surprised. Lisa shrugged. "I googled it." Kim nodded, impressed, but she was still pissed. They headed over to Theo's manager's office and walked in. They waited in the lobby for at least fifteen minutes. Then David came out and greeted them.

"Hello, ladies. Sorry for the wait. Just taking care of a little business." David looked perplexed by them calling and showing up. They all walked in David's office.

"So, David, how are you doing? I heard so much about you," Kim said.

"And you too, Kim."

"This is my daughter, Lisa."

"Hello," Lisa said with a cordial smile.

"Hello, Lisa. So what can I help you guys with?"

"I am trying to get in touch with Theo," Kim explained.

"Well, he's doing an interview. He should be finished in a couple of hours."

"Oh."

"Is something wrong?"

"No," Kim replied.

"Actually there is. Theo asked my mom to marry him last night. And this morning I read about his little contract problem with his publisher, courtesy of Jordan Yikes. He just wants to marry my mom to fulfill his stupid contract. If he doesn't, he loses his publishing deal." Lisa folded her arms. "But I guess you know all that."

"As you could can see, she might end up in your business one day," Kim said.

"I was about to say the same thing."

"She wants to go to law school."

"Where?"

"Stanford," Kim said, proud.

"Great school," David said.

Lisa wasn't impressed with the small talk.

"Look, I just want to talk to him. 'Cause I don't want to be used," Kim's eyes showed she was hurt.

David smiled. Kim and Lisa looked at each other baffled by his amusement. "Well, it looks like we're both pissed off at Theo. You wanna know why I'm pissed?" The two ladies looked at him confused.

Theo ran through the streets of New York City in the rain and straight into the building where his book publisher had his offices. It was late, so most of the people who worked there were leaving or already gone.

Once inside, he saw his publisher, Larry Becker, talking to his employees in the conference room. Larry saw him through the big plate glass windows and signaled him to come inside. Theo entered a room full of well-dressed people wearing smiles, including Larry.

"Well, look who came to say hello. Our star client, Theodore Washington."

Theo gave an uncomfortable smile. Some of the people looked impressed, some didn't.

"Hello, everybody. Uh, Larry, can I talk to you for a minute? Private."

"Theo, we're all friends here. What's on your mind?"

Theo thought for a moment, looking at some of the smug expressions in the room.

"Look, I just wanted to tell you that I won't be getting married because of some woman's threats. I'm bigger than that. When I get married, I'm getting married for love. Not for a book contract."

Larry smiled, amused by Theo's naive notion of love.

"Take it from me, Theo, love is overrated. I've seen it all. And a book contract will actually make you money instead of costing you money. Trust me, I know. I've been married four times," Larry said with a sarcastic chuckle.

"I'm happy for you, but I'm only planning to get married once."

"Good for you. But like I told you before, I'm not honoring your contract without you getting married. It would be like a financial adviser selling his book while he's in bankruptcy."

"Or an asshole giving marital advice," Theo said, almost like a reflex.

Everyone's eyes went wide.

"Look, I'd rather lose everything I have than be controlled by some stupid contract. Or stupid person."

"I hope you're talking about Jordan Yikes?"

"You figure it out." Theo turned and walked toward the door. Larry turned red, feeling embarrassed in front of his employees.

"You can just forget about your contract altogether."

"I already did. So fuck you, Larry Becker," Theo said matter-of-factly, wearing freedom in his expression. He looked around the room at the people with their mouths wide open. He then addressed everyone, one by one.

"And fuck you. You all right. And fuck you. You cool. Fuck you and you. You're awesome. And fuck all of you guys back there."

Some looked offended and some amused. Some were even impressed. He addressed Larry.

"You don't control people. You only employ them. I am my own man. I decide my fate, not you."

The people in the room continued to stare dumbfounded.

"Somebody call security," Larry stammered.

"No need," Theo replied as he strolled out wearing a satisfied smile as Larry stood there emasculated.

When David finished telling them what had happened, Kim's and Lisa's eyes were glazed over. They were deeply touched. David smiled. They smiled back.

"Theo is a good man," David said in admiration of his friend.

"I know," Kim and Lisa said at the same time.

Kim exhaled with a chuckle, then said, "Can you not mention our little visit?"

David gave a laugh.

"Well, he is my friend and client, so normally I tell him everything. But in this case, he doesn't need to know."

Kim sat there wearing a silly smile. Lisa grabbed her mother's hand, smiling as well.

Chapter 40

EIGHT MONTHS LATER THEO'S HOUSE WAS FULL OF people. They walked in and out, dressed for a wedding. A *For Sale* sign graced the front yard.

Kim's kids ran through the house. Xavier looked dapper in a black tuxedo. Lisa and Christiahn wore beautiful lavender dresses.

"Hurry, you guys!" Lisa said. Lisa felt her phone vibrate in her purse. There was an email sent to her that stopped her in her tracks. It was from Kevin. He simply wrote *I am so sorry for what I did. It was childish and mean. Kevin.* She thought for a moment, then a hint of a smile crossed her lips.

Lisa and the kids scurried downstairs, and a few family members headed out back with them. The back doors opened to a beautiful garden wedding, full of floral decorations.

The guests sat in white chairs, waiting for the wedding to begin. Margie smiled at the sight of the three kids running out of the house.

Theo, Sam, David and three other men waited at the huge white altar. David leaned over to Sam. "God damn, that's a lot of kids!" he said with a smirk.

"Who you tellin'? And it'll be five soon," Sam added. They chuckled. Theo heard them and smiled.

"That's right, five. My favorite number. Now shut the fuck up before I kick both your asses."

"All right, all right," David said.

The groomsmen laughed, as people hurried to grab their seats.

"By the way, it would have been nice to just go to Vegas. Strippers, gambling, and weddings. That's what it's known for," David added.

"I told you. She doesn't like Vegas. And there wasn't no... rush." Theo said with an ironic smile.

The organ played *Here Comes The Bride*. Everyone turned toward the back of the garden. Xavier and Christiahn threw rose petals on the ground as they walked to the alter. However, they got into a fight and had to be pulled apart.

The bridesmaids came down, one by one. Kim came down last, Margie at her side. Her belly was huge and she looked beautiful. Margie led her to the altar and handed her over to Theo. Theo and Margie shared a warm smile.

Kim and Theo stood side by side in front of the preacher. The two said their vows, then exchanged wedding rings. Family and friends looked on with joy.

The newly married couple kissed, sealing the deal, making their union official. The kids smiled, seeing their mother the happiest they'd ever seen her.

They partied in the backyard, dancing, having a good time. As the night went on and people left, the family continued to dance as if the reception was in full swing. They had more fun with only the family on the dance floor.

Sam and David sat watching from afar, having a drink. They clinked their glasses, wearing smiles, proud of Theo.

Margie talked to a handsome gentleman in his early sixties. He gave her his card. Their eyes flirted as they drank their wine.

Theo's mother and father sat watching, proud as well. When they got up and danced, Kim saw them and hugged them both.

Theo danced, smiling from ear to ear with his three kids and pregnant wife, happy as hell.

That night Theo sat on his back porch by himself, still in his tuxedo, his shirt partly unbuttoned and shoes off. He drank a glass of wine while smoking a cigar. Kim was upstairs sleeping for three, the twins in her belly. Theo texted back and forth on his phone. He got up, curious. He put on his shoes and strolled down the side of his house, out to the front. A Honda Accord was parked across the street. He walked over to it and got in. Coco sat there glowing, beautiful as ever. They smiled and hugged.

"You look happy," Coco said.

"You do, too."

"I hope it's okay I dropped by. I just wanted to say goodbye in person, being that I probably won't see you again." She had a sadness in her eyes even though she was smiling.

"I'm glad you did. How are you?"

"I'm fine. I just wanted to be as appropriate as possible, that's why I waited so late. That doesn't sound right. I figured you'd be the only one still up. Being that you write late at night."

"Hey, I was up," he said. "It is good to see you."

"I just wanted to say I'm moving back home to Atlanta and living with my grandmother. I'm going to get out of the dating business for good. I'm going to go to junior college. Try to find myself. Set some goals." She laughed.

"That sounds great."

"You know it's because of you, right?"

Theo stared at her, touched, swallowing the lump in his throat.

"You inspire me to be better. Hell, you gave up your book contract for that woman in there. That takes a special person."

"Well, I just hope my finances work out."

"It'll be fine. I learned that from you." She kissed him on the cheek. "So, thank you."

"You're welcome."

They smiled. Then hugged again.

"You're going to be great, you know that?" Theo said.

"I know," she said, confident.

Theo smiled, got out of the car and closed the door. The window rolled down.

"Oh, by the way. I handled that writer chick for you."

"What?" He looked inside the window.

In a flash we see Coco dressed in her ghetto fabulous best, with Jordan in a headlock in front of her house.

"I'm going to do this every time I see you bad mouthing my friend, you hear bitch? So stay off *YouTube* or I'm going to put me fucking you up on *YouTube* every week! You got that?"

"Oh my God! Somebody help me!" Jordan yelled.

"Do you understand me?" Coco reiterated, squeezing her neck.

"Yeah, jeeze!"

"Don't make me come find you, or next time I'mma really put it on that ass."

"I promise." Jordan cried out.

"You better, 'cause I'll have every gangsta bitch in the city looking for you! You heard?"

"I hear you!"

Coco let Jordan go. She looked more shooked and embarrassed than anything. She saw a few of her neighbors outside looking at her strangely, shaking their heads in a disapproving fashion. Jordan rushed back into her house and slammed the door shut.

Theo looked stunned. "You know gangsta bitches? I thought you didn't know anybody out here."

"I don't. I was bluffin'."

"You didn't hurt her?" Theo asked concerned.

"Hell no. I'm not trying to go to jail. Hell, I start school next month. Anyway, you won't be having any more problems with her."

Theo looked amazed.

"I got you, boo," she said adoringly. She smiled and winked, blew a kiss and drove off. He watched her drive down the street in awe. Then cracked a smile.

He strolled back to his backyard and sat in his chair with his feet up. He thought about what he learned over the last nine months. And how although it was good to have a plan, the journey itself is truly the best part of life. And the curveballs are the lessons. Like his friend Sam said, *You just have to follow your heart, 'cause life is too short to make mistakes you know you're making.*

Chapter 41

THREE MONTHS LATER, THE WASHINGTONS LIVED IN Kim's crammed house with all five kids. Their lives were chaotic with screaming twins. Theo changed the boy's diaper while Kim changed the girl's. The girl's name was Olivia and the boy's was Theo, Jr.

Two years later Theo's family entered their new house. It resembled his old home—big and beautiful with a Victorian-style exterior.

Margie and Lisa held the twins. Lisa smiled brightly, wearing a Stanford University sweatshirt. Kim was wearing her cap and gown. Inside the house was a big banner stretched across the wall that read *Congratulations, Kim!*

Kim smiled at the sight of it and hugged Theo. They all applauded her. She felt like she was on top of the world, accomplishing something she never dreamed she would. She made it through the fire, and knew she was stronger because of it. She smiled brightly, almost giddy, feeling the love of her family.

Theo's eyes got watery, overwhelmed with emotion by the wonderful moment they were all sharing. Tears flowed down his cheeks. He quickly wiped his tears away, a little embarrassed, but Kim stopped him grabbing both of his hands. They laughed, as she stared into his eyes knowing there is no shame in tears.

Two months later Kim went to her mailbox. Among the envelopes was a *Writer's Digest* magazine with Theo on the cover holding his new book with his family. The book was titled *Five Steps To Family*. The subtitle: *How Theo Self-Published His New Book, Making Him a Millionaire.*

She walked into the family room and handed Theo the magazine, wearing a huge smile. He beamed, looking at the cover. She sat in his lap, giving him a loving kiss. She sighed, laying her head in his chest, taking in their new home and new life together. They were soulmates in love, happy to have accomplished their goals, and looking forward to the journey together that lay ahead.

Kim scanned the wall behind them with a group of Theo's college degrees on it. The last one was Kim's *Bachelor of Science in Economics* from *UCLA*.

Kim smiled proudly and so did Theo. He looked at her and thought, *Damn I love this woman.*

The End